INVITATION
TO ALL COUPLES IN LOVE

We, the citizens of Eternity, take great pleasure in inviting you to hold your wedding at the Powell Chapel.

Remember the legend: Those who exchange their vows in the chapel will remain together for the rest of their lives.

So let us help plan your special day. We've been making dreams come true for more than a hundred years.

Weddings, Inc.
Eternity, Massachusetts

Weddings, Inc.

Join us every month
in Eternity, Massachusetts...where love lasts forever.

If you miss any of these WEDDINGS, INC. stories, get in touch with Harlequin Reader Service:

In the U.S.

3010 Walden Avenue
P.O. Box 1369
Buffalo, NY 14269-1369

In Canada

P.O. Box 609
Fort Erie, Ontario
L2A 5X3

SARA WOOD

The Vengeful Groom

Harlequin Books

TORONTO • NEW YORK • LONDON
AMSTERDAM • PARIS • SYDNEY • HAMBURG
STOCKHOLM • ATHENS • TOKYO • MILAN
MADRID • WARSAW • BUDAPEST • AUCKLAND

Sara Wood is acknowledged as
the author of this work.

ISBN 0-373-11692-6

THE VENGEFUL GROOM

Copyright © 1994 by Harlequin Enterprises B.V.

This edition published by arrangement with Harlequin Enterprises B. V.

® and TM are trademarks of the publisher. Trademarks indicated with ® are registered in the United States Patent and Trademark Office, the Canadian Trade Marks Office and in other countries.

Printed in U.S.A.

Weddings, Inc.
DIRECTORY

Your guide to the perfect Happily-Ever-After

Dear Reader,

When I left my home near Plymouth, England, and flew across the Atlantic to Massachusetts to research *The Vengeful Groom,* I imagined myself as nervous as any Pilgrim. I found woodlands, clapboard houses, glorious beaches and historic inns. "English" scenery, and yet everything felt so foreign.

I filmed, I researched, I learned a new language. Pudding is dessert, estate agents are Realtors, cafés are diners.... I also walked in Giovanni and Tina's footsteps, living their lives, dreaming on beaches, talking to students, exploring mansions, a garage and small-town life. I visited Harvard and Boston's Italian quarter.

There was also time for playing hooky—wandering the wilder shores of Cape Cod, boating up silvery rivers and across vast salt marshlands. At Plymouth Plantation, I told a costumed carpenter that he'd find old Plymouth much changed if he went back! We drew maps for each other in the dirt and talked about the Old World and the New.

I wasn't as daring as the settlers who'd made the journey from England long ago, but I felt an affinity with them. I'd come from a great distance, with high hopes of adventure and a broadening of my world. I gained a deep respect and admiration for the American way of life—for its energy and enthusiasm and family values.

I think we need those strong, caring qualities in a marriage; Giovanni and Tina have them in *The Vengeful Groom*— a tough grit, a regard for family and a "can do" attitude. With a never-dying love for each other, they'll be happy together for eternity. Hope you agree!

With affection,

Sara Wood

CHAPTER ONE

SHE OUGHT to go over there. Even a Lamborghini could break down—otherwise why would that guy be lying underneath it? Tina shut the apartment door, mesmerized by the seductive lines of the dark green automobile on the derelict lot next door. From beneath the megasize front bumper emerged a pair of leather shoes and a small pool of oil.

Man at work, she thought in amusement, and there was the obligatory crowd—almost a dozen students! Though why the guy had run the car up the clamshell path and parked by the ruined barn, she couldn't imagine. Her grandfather's garage stood within pushing distance.

With a quick gesture, she thrust back the disorderly chunks of black hair that had flopped into her eyes from the dash downstairs and contemplated leaving the Lamborghini owner to cope. A slow smile curved the poppy red of her mouth as she speculated on the shock the poor guy must be in!

She *could* ignore his predicament since her grandfather had ordered her to concentrate on her own pleasures for once and let everything else go hang. Since he'd taken Adriana away on an extended birthday treat, the weekend didn't involve planning a whole heap of the enriching experiences Adriana needed if she was to progress. Although Tina loved them—from the hilarious cooking sessions at breakfast to the stories she read at night to help Adriana unwind—it meant she never had a moment to herself.

Today she was as free as a bird, with nothing to concern her but which pickle to put on her sandwich. She'd felt a little guilty, a little lost, that morning. Scrambling into her

T-shirt and shorts, she'd realized she needn't hurry for once. No dependents. No detailed planning. No mental exertion. No dealing with emotional dramas. Bliss!

Seven-fifteen. The part-timers would arrive at the garage in half an hour. And business was business. She clambered over the picket fence and strolled toward the students.

"Hi, everyone," she called amiably.

"Hi, Miss Murphy!" they answered with enthusiasm.

She beamed back and found she had to stretch all of her curvy five-foot-two frame to get a glimpse of the low-slung auto above the milling heads.

"Are you guys studying chiropody this term, or is this a customer for my grandpa?" she asked, nodding in amusement at the leather soles sticking out from beneath the car. To her surprise, the feet wagged as if they enjoyed the feeble joke.

"More'n that, Miss Murphy! Come see!" cried Josh Davis, good-naturedly shoving his neighbors in all directions to clear a space for her.

"Oh, boy!" she murmured in approval, running a connoisseur's eye over the auto. It would snarl and roar and overtake everything in sight, leaving a choking cloud of dust behind. She smiled. "Grandpa will *die* to hear he's missed it!"

"Yeah. Awesome," breathed Josh. "It's a Countach! Smooth!"

"As silk," she agreed fervently, her fingers reaching out with due respect to stroke the satiny finish on the curvaceous bodywork. She loved to touch sensuous objects. She leaned over and sniffed the leather interior. Wonderfully evocative. And then she frowned faintly. Cream linen pants weren't the most likely gear for wriggling under low-slung cars. How very odd.

It dawned on her that Mr. Rich-in-Trouble had chosen that spot in the sunken path of the garden so he could shoehorn himself beneath the hood and work on the underside. Doing what? she wondered, a little baffled over the limited possibilities. Intrigued, she studied the pool of oil and concluded that it looked rather...arranged.

Lisa Powell distracted her from the mystery. "And sexy," she sighed dreamily. "Moves like molasses."

"The car?" murmured Tina dryly.

"No! Him." Lisa sighed, gazing at the few inches of linen-clad shins as though she coveted everything above and below. "Sex appeal," she announced with all the assurance of a sixteen-year-old, "is a matter of body language. And eyes that melt tarmac."

"No wonder he's got a hole in his car," said Tina gravely. The students all laughed and the feet did their annoying jiggle. "Since you never mentioned you've got X-ray vision on your profile forms for college, Lisa," she added with a grin, "I suppose you watched the guy slide under there."

"Yes, and wait till he slides out again!" Lisa gloated. "He's very exotic. Or do I mean erotic? And his hair is the most extraordinary white-blond..."

Giovanni, Tina thought at once, his name shocking her with its sudden arrival in her head. Giovanni moved with an undeniably erotic grace, and his hair sat like whipped cream on his tanned Latin forehead, making a startling contrast.

Back came that star-burst moment when she'd fallen so helplessly in love with him. He'd walked into her class when she was an impressionable fourteen and he'd been a year older—a tall, graceful Polish-Sicilian from the back streets of Palermo, with pride and apprehension and defiance fighting in his expression.

"I prefer dark guys myself," she stated emphatically, wrinkling her small nose.

"How's it goin', sir?" called Josh respectfully to the feet and cream pants.

"Great."

The muffled reply came as a relief because it meant she didn't need to hang around. But she couldn't help wishing he was some rich guy who'd turned up to buy the garage. Then her grandfather could retire and stop creaking himself into gear every morning. Even with the part-timers and guys on school placement sharing the work, he ended up exhausted. Having Adriana around with her innocent demands didn't help, however much happiness she brought.

Tina's expression grew soft and affectionate when she scanned the small Murphy's Garage, with their cramped apartment above and a For Sale sign in front. Then her gaze returned to the burned-out buildings of the derelict Alden place a few yards away. Brent Powell—now Josh's stepfather, she reminded herself—had nearly lost his life in the fire there a couple of years ago. A terrible scene, an awful memory.

It was a scandal that the old colonial house and outbuildings were still standing in ruins and that the town couldn't enforce the destruction order. The place was an eyesore, and the blackened timbers and collapsing clapboard facade had badly affected Grandpa's asking price.

And then she gave a wry grin. She'd promised Grandpa she wouldn't think of anyone but herself today, and already she'd checked on a crowd of students and a tinkering Lamborghini driver, and worried about selling the garage!

"Well, if everything's okay, I'm off to pick up a picnic for the beach," she said cheerfully. "Hang around, you guys. Awed hayseeds sometimes get dimes thrown to them!"

Lisa giggled. "I'm not going! Bet you'd stay, too, if you were sixteen."

"You got it!" Tina admitted. "But I'm more than ten years beyond that sell-by date!" She grinned, knowing how old that must seem to Lisa. "Only a senior citizen with a decent pension would give me a passing glance now."

Something hit her small sandaled foot. A silver coin. She blinked. "What the . . . ?"

Everyone was laughing. "A dime for a hayseed, Miss Murphy!"

"It's his pension—you hit the jackpot!" cried Josh.

"Then he's got sound judgment," she said simply.

The blueness of her eyes deepened with warmth at their laughter. She loved it that they could crack jokes together and that they regarded her as a friend. The relationship she'd evolved with them over the years had gotten to be as comfortable and familiar as an old sofa. Too comfortable sometimes, she thought ruefully; the students seemed to think she was available all hours of the day—and night. But then, they knew she'd move heaven and earth for them and she'd root for them till she dropped. Though, come a crunch, she could do some tough talking and deal with a drama or two.

A second coin landed on her red-painted toe. Fascinated, she pushed her hands into the pockets of her shorts. Skillful, she thought. He didn't have much room to maneuver under there.

"I'm being targeted," she marveled. "Hey. I'm a high school guidance counselor, not a slot machine!"

"He's pretty accurate," Brad Phister said admiringly.

"Perhaps he pitches for the Red Sox," she suggested.

Feeling curious, she crouched down, tipping her head sideways in an attempt to see under the car. She got a view of a male body clad in discreetly toned cream, a hunky quarterback chest soaring up and preventing her from seeing beyond, and a bared flexing arm and the flesh of a gold watch as another silver coin whizzed in her direction.

"Hi, there! You practicing stone skipping?" No answer. "Okay, I give up. What *are* you doing? Try dollar bills! I take credit cards! Gold!" she called, unable to keep the laughter from her voice. It was crazy! The guy still didn't answer, and she stood up in puzzled defeat.

Then the glove-soft shoes shot forward, the girls taking in a collective breath as the long legs and slim hips of a young, athletic-looking male came into view. Rich, too, thought Tina, highly intrigued. Those immaculately pressed pants weren't from a thrift shop. Her curiosity soared as questions of who, why and what skated around her brain.

Under her fascinated gaze, the discreet cream knees bent and the leather-clad heels propelled the body out a little more. Now they could all see that the guy had been lying on a proper mechanic's trolley. The mystery deepened. A trolley wasn't the kind of thing a rich man kept handy.

"I think he's Italian," stated Lisa, "despite the blond hair. Wait till you see his pecs!"

"Pecs? I've seen pecs," said Tina mildly, but she stayed nevertheless, dying to know why a blond Italian would throw coins....

She took a step back in shock. Her small hand went to her brightly painted mouth. A blond Italian. Italian car. Italian shoes.

Oh, God!

Her skin paled beneath its tan, washed with gray from head to toe, her huge, dark-lashed eyes suddenly great sinking navy pools in her horrified face. Suddenly she didn't want to stay around the dime-tossing stranger any longer. Just in case. Her heart stopped beating for a brief moment as the ground seemed to heave beneath her feet and she tried to steady herself.

It could well be Giovanni.

Hazily she focused on the feet, the legs, the dancer-slim hips. It *couldn't* be. No, some other guy. Why had she thought of Gio? Her intuition had gone crazy. He could never afford to rent a Lamborghini, let alone buy one. Surely... She swallowed. No man in his position would want to come back. The shame, the accusing stares, the stony silence from everyone would be unbearable for him.

Yet there was the familiar thud in her chest that came when Giovanni was close, the melting of her body into a molten heap, ready to erupt when he touched her, spoke, fixed her with his brooding, heavy-lidded eyes.

Since his departure so long ago, nothing had changed the way she felt deep inside. A crowd of guys had dated her; a few had kissed her. She scowled, firmly pushing back the inevitable thought that none of them had taken her all the way to heaven the way Giovanni had.

Perhaps it was just as well. The lush red of her lips parted in a grimace of pain. Never again in her entire life did she want to feel that she was dying inside because of a man's rejection and his casual betrayal. Or to realize that the man she'd loved was without honor or backbone. No wonder Gio's adoring parents had disowned him!

She inhaled sharply, slamming the door on a pain ten years old. That was how you dealt with tragedy; when it was too huge, too hurtful to cope with, you eliminated it from your mind and threw yourself into work one hundred percent and made some kind of a life for yourself.

Her mouth trembled. Every now and then, a word, a gesture, the angle of a jaw or a word spoken on the television, caused her to learn the cruel lesson that her love for Giovanni had never faded; it was merely suppressed. Which made her a mindless fool, because only a mindless fool carried a torch for a cheat and a liar.

Men like Gio were virtually programmed to build up a woman's hopes, to deceive and disappoint—then to vanish. He was a coward. No, worse than that, she thought unhappily. Much worse. As bad as a man could be.

She pressed a trembling hand against the cerulean blue of her T-shirt. Beneath her soft breath, her heart beat in an alarmingly erratic rhythm.

"Miss Murphy? You okay?"

"I...oh, too many waffles for breakfast," she told Brad, taking a quick gulp of oxygen to fill her crushed lungs. "I'll give the pecs a miss. They're a dime a dozen now that everyone works out," she continued hurriedly. "Ask him if they do Countachs in a ragtop!" Her attempt to sound casual began to fall apart. The feet and legs had edged forward ultraslowly, and the beefy torso was being revealed in all its masculine glory. Giovanni, her brain told her. "Have fun, you guys! Gotta go!" She whirled around, striding fast as a whippet toward the street.

To her acutely tuned ears came the rasping sound of trolley wheels on the clamshells. She hastily flung open the drunken gate and strode onto the sidewalk. "There's no earthly reason that it should be him!" she muttered to herself. "None at all—"

"Teeenaaa!"

"Ohhhh!" she gasped.

Quickening her pace, she pretended she didn't recognize the rich, rolling, elaborately drawn-out extension of the syllables of her name. But no one in the world except Giovanni had the ability to caress even the most ordinary word. Those lilting cadences, a rough edge and an Italian's way with women had given him advantages over other men, and the easily won adoration had flawed him fatally. Women came willingly to his arms, she thought, sick at heart.

"Teeenaaa!"

Grim faced, she faked deafness and forged on till a painfully remembered musical whistle stopped her as dead as if she'd hit a brick wall. *Their call!*

Their secret call, when they'd needed one another. How could he? How *could* he? Emotions coursed through her in destructive waves. Love. Regret. Shame. Anger. And contempt by the bucket. Too much to cope with. Tina got her leaden feet working again, her mind still in turmoil. Giovanni! Not in a million years had she expected to see him again—or ever wanted to!

Why had he come? Her dazed mind whirled, seeking an explanation for his hiring an ostentatious car when it was unlikely he could afford such extravagances. He'd never made it to college, and there'd been that period in... Tina's white teeth savaged her lower lip as she fought to keep her emotions under control. Jail. She'd said it. Jail had taken up two years of his life. Not much opportunity to make money with that track record.

Reluctantly she faced the truth she'd been avoiding. He'd sworn he'd return one day—and make everyone sit up and take notice.

An image burned itself in her mind. She closed her eyes briefly in anguish, but the image was even clearer, and when she snapped them open again he was still there—in court, just after the sentence had been read, his eyes flickering in malediction between her and her once-dear friend Beth, because they'd provided the evidence that had damned him.

"I'll be back!" he'd yelled across the courtroom, her heart breaking at the way he'd struggled with the restraining officer. The hurt racked through her now and then; Gio had protested his innocence to the last and never admitted his guilt. "I swear to God you'll all know when I've hit town!"

Ashen faced, Tina stepped up her pace, driving her wobbling legs toward the café a few hundred yards down the street. She wished it wasn't Saturday, because only a handful of people were stirring—mainly students and those like herself who'd become accustomed to getting up for school at seven-thirty. She wanted crowds. The safety of numbers and friendly faces because that day in court was one she wanted to forget forever. And suddenly it was here and now, and she couldn't bear it.

The whistle sounded again, louder, more imperious, as though she'd turn and run to him like some obedient dog. Her heart tripped a beat. He'd called her a bitch of the first order, his eyes glittering with hatred, the promise of retribution in every inch of his powerful body.

Sicilian vengeance. Cold, calculated, final.

And now he was here. Giovanni, having been brought up a Sicilian half his life, would be nursing a grudge he would take to the grave if it wasn't satisfied. The past swept relentlessly into the present: everything she'd seen and felt that day in court, Gio's black malevolent eyes, staring, condemning, the nervous sips she'd taken of the water they'd given her when her voice had failed, the physical sickness. . . .

The wave of nausea now made her stumble. Hot, sweating, she recovered, thrust her hand through her hair and plunged blindly on. She'd gotten to the bank. Nearly up to the bridge, the café, the haven that lay inside.

By the time she crested the old bridge she was out of breath and could feel his presence close behind her like an evil force. Suddenly her legs lost their ability to move and her feet just gave up. She hung on to the parapet wall and looked down at her legs in bewilderment, willing them to obey her. Failing.

"Ciao, Tina," Giovanni murmured, so softly, so slowly it could break a woman's heart. "Ciao."

Small flurries of nerves rippled right down to her bare and wriggling toes. The punch of pure delight had knocked her brain away and left space for her sensuality to flow unheeded. Her small hands screwed into tight hurting balls, because the old magic was still there despite everything he'd done, and her whole emotional inner world had roared into life. Tina gritted her teeth against the long-forgotten ability of her brain and physical body to melt when his voice caressed her in that sexy indolent way. It was nothing but a memory quirk. A cruel reflex action.

"*Arrivederci!*" she flung behind her shakily.

"Turn around, Tina. *Allora,* turn to me."

The warm, languid and silken voice slid over her shoulder, shivering up her sensitive neck and then crawling over every inch of her body. And the memories flooded back like the remorseless tide, washing away all her flimsy barriers and leaving her stranded, high and dry, with only one focus. Giovanni.

Weakly she lifted her face to the early-morning warmth of the sun, and she could almost feel his firm dreamy mouth on hers, teaching her how to kiss, how to enjoy her body without shame. Dark with anger, her eyes narrowed. Of course he'd taught her that! Look what he'd gotten in return!

"I don't want to see you. Or speak to you," she said huskily. "I'm on my way to the café." She was afraid, unwilling to look him in the eye. This was the man she'd loved, ached for. Betrayed.

"You might as well face me," he drawled. "You can't run from your mistakes forever."

Stunned, she whirled around, every inch of her quivering with the injustice of his remark, her Irish temper flaring as she tasted in her throat the bitterness of her error in giving her love to a sham.

"*You* were my mistake, Gio! You were a mistake!" she cried incoherently. "It was a mistake that you were ever born!'' With that, her hand swept up and connected with his sardonic mocking face in a resounding crack that went right through her, shuddering down into her bones. She uttered one strangled broken cry of horrified remorse and turned, planning to run, her mind reeling from the terrible image of Giovanni's savage mouth, his malefic eyes, her fingers tingling from the electric sensation when they'd connected with warm satin skin clothing the rock of his jaw.

A huge hand closed on her slender arm, stopping her with its crushing force before she'd taken one faltering step. ''That slap, Tina,'' he said with a dangerous softness, ''was your mistake.''

''Take your hand off me!'' she said jerkily. Being touched by him was a shock. They were joined again, the tension between them firing her with a sensation of uncontainable volcanic energy. Appalled, she tugged at his hand, but it only tightened, drawing her closer, and she knew with sinking heart that she'd have to look in his accusing eyes again and face the situation.

She could deal with this. She wasn't a guileless teenager any longer. She had a track record of dealing with trouble. Anyone who could handle unwanted pregnancies, knife fights and anxious parents could pull herself together and show a bit of cool in a crisis.

This was nothing, she told herself, but knew she lied, because she was emotionally involved and it wasn't the same at all.

''I won't release you yet. First, I have something for you, Tina,'' he muttered. And he twisted her around, impaling her with his black, black eyes.

The white imprint of her hand flared accusingly against the dark gold of his skin, and she stared at the mark of her contempt as if hypnotized by it.

''You have nothing for me,'' she said in a low tone.

He had changed. Bigger, harder, with a hatred that lay cold as ice in the cruel eyes. Yet whatever the hardships he'd suffered, there was still that stomach-clenching impact of stunning good looks. Blond hair on a dark-skinned Sicilian had thrown a curve at women of all tastes and ages, and she'd never been immune. Her mouth trembled with a soft exhalation.

"I have," he murmured. "More than you think."

"Only memories, Giovanni," she replied quietly.

The songs they'd sung on clambakes, the trips down the Sussex River in a flat-bottomed boat, the lazy days building sand castles on Neck Beck. The laughter. The affection. Licking each other's sticky fingers—and then the doughnut sugar off Giovanni's lips....

Tina drew in a quick breath, her expression guilty because she'd become aware that she was being watched by a pair of melting eyes that gleamed like deep shaded water—black, still and fathomless—and the mark on his face had grown into an angry red. His expression chilled her to the bone.

"Done all the checking you're going to do?" he murmured sardonically. "Have I changed so much?"

She shrugged and pretended that was what she was still doing, quite surprised at his sophistication and casually elegant clothes. Yet in the rawness of his wicked eyes lay hints of that exciting rough edge of danger, which also touched his carnal mouth and made her think carnal thoughts.

"Little change," she said huskily. "You still have the arrogance to imagine women will come whenever you call." Her head lifted in defiance. "Let me go, or I'm going to scream."

His eyes narrowed. The steady pull of his hand brought her close enough to feel his hot breath flaming her hot skin. His finger had delicately scooped up a bead of sweat from her forehead and transferred it to his tongue before she could blink. But the effect devastated her; all the sensual pleasures they'd enjoyed had turned her into a voluptuary, and that one small gesture filled her body with a terrible ache. He smiled with triumph when she remained mute, nursing her desolation.

"I need five minutes of your time," he said, his black eyes unreadable. "Nothing more. Yet."

Five minutes. She could survive that and wipe him from her life again. "What do you want?" she demanded shortly.

The extravagant mouth eased into a cynical smile. "You left these behind just now. They're yours. Multiply them by ten," he drawled, "and you get thirty pieces of silver."

And before she knew what he intended, he'd reached out and pulled forward the neck of her thin T-shirt with a disdainful thumb and forefinger, audaciously dumping the three dimes into the gap. They lay stuck to her sweating breasts and stomach, dust and dirt and bits of clamshell and all.

"You brute!" she gasped in red-faced outrage as he calmly dusted off his hands and wiped them on an immaculate navy silk handkerchief. "You've made me feel dirty inside!"

The corners of his mouth swooped downward in scorn and he tucked the handkerchief back in his jacket pocket. "But, Tina," he demurred, "I thought you were already dirty inside."

She winced. "I'm clean scrubbed," she said tightly, easing her top from the waistband of her shorts and letting the coins fall to the ground. Then she concentrated on trying to dislodge the bits from her stomach by rubbing vigorously—till she realized from the breathless silence, and then his frowning stare, what the movement was doing to her unsupported breasts.

"You look pretty pure," he conceded laconically. "But there's no honor or loyalty in there." His scornful finger stabbed the air, pointing at her heart. "And when you drop the demure act, we get the truth. A woman driven by sex who's only too ready to launch into a display of erotic originality."

Tina was momentarily lost for words. Slowly her expressive eyes widened, their color first pale, then becoming almost navy as her emotions changed from shock to shame and then to outrage.

"Hypocrite!" she said bitterly. "I thought that we had a loving relationship and that our lovemaking was the natural consequence of our affection. I wasn't ashamed of sharing my body with you—then. I am deeply shamed by it now!" she said shakily. "I trusted you with my most precious secrets...and you tricked me! All my life I'll resent you for taking my innocence and betraying it when it had been so gladly, so devotedly given as a gift for the man I loved!"

"Do you hold me solely responsible for your seduction?" he drawled.

Tina lowered her head. She blamed herself for trusting him. "I—I was innocent and I didn't know I was..."

"Getting me beyond the point of no return?" he suggested. "So was I to blame for finding you irresistible, or were you to blame for not realizing how naive and provocative your behavior was to a teenager with Sicilian blood?"

"We were both to blame," she said quietly.

"Progress at last," he mocked. "There's always shared blame, Tina. Remember that. Hold it in your beautiful head and think about it. And remember we were in love," he said softly, as though remembering with pleasure. *"Love."*

Heat scoured through her, head to toe, making her skin prickle. Shaken by the warmth in his voice, the lyrical indolence that cruelly brought back the soft nights beneath the stars and the moonlight gleaming on their naked skin, she let her thick black lashes hide the desolate expression in her eyes. If only she'd never let him arouse her to that fateful point of no return! It had been such a corny error to make after hearing the magic words, *I love you.* He loved himself. Sex. Her teeth snagged at her lip, stilling its tremble.

"Take the coins," he said tightly. "They represent your betrayal," he said, slivers of steel behind each carefully enunciated word.

She winced. "What did you want me to do in court? Stay silent? Perjure myself?" she asked, her voice husky with emotion, because she'd considered those options but obeyed her conscience.

"I wanted you to believe me," he replied quietly.

"It wasn't possible!" she cried irritably. "I know what I saw. Please, Gio. Don't let's go over it again. It was bad enough the first time. What benefit is there in raking up the past and accusing one another? Let it be!'' she pleaded.

"I can't." He seemed unaware that his hands were lightly sweeping up and down her bare arms. His eyes impaled hers, blazing a message she didn't understand. "I wish I could walk away right now," he said huskily. "But the memories have drawn me back, and I can't escape them any longer."

Nor could she. All she could think of right now was what it would be like to be in his embrace again, clasped to the big curves of his muscular body. She felt a flash of fire deep within her slumbering core, and she tensed, her hands curling like claws to stop her maverick fingers from humiliating her by touching him. He had to go. Now, before she said or did something she'd regret for the rest of her life. She had regrets enough.

"You must leave town," she said flatly. "Or..."

"Or what?" he murmured. "You'll call the police and claim I harassed you?"

"I don't want to, Gio. But push me and I might," she muttered.

"I'd be arrested."

Her head tipped high. "Not if you left," she pointed out.

"You'd get me into trouble again just because you can't cope with your own sexual response to me?" he asked in clipped tones. "Like the last time?"

He showed no shame, no guilt, no recognition that he'd been in the wrong. Tina felt the color in her face drain away, the beat of her pulse ticking like a time bomb.

"The evidence was overwhelming," she rasped. "You drove your car on the night of the accident. You kept denying it and you're still stubbornly denying it, but I saw you and so did dozens of others, and there is no doubt in my mind that you drove the car that...that..." She choked, but forced herself to say it, however much it hurt. "That killed my sister—and her baby!" she finished hoarsely.

And she felt her heart jerk in pain, remembering the last time she'd seen her sister, Sue, and her baby, Michael, alive—she and Sue splattered with apple-and-banana puree, laughing fondly at little Mikey's determined attempts to feed himself. A sob rose in her throat, choking her, and she gritted her teeth to hold back the threatening tears.

Gio's lips had whitened in anger. "How could you believe that? I'll never understand...." he said, shaking his head.

"Beth said—" she began miserably.

"Didn't it matter what I had to say?" he asked roughly. "Wasn't I owed any loyalty? I was your lover. You were supposed to be in love with me and I deserved a hearing. You gave me none! How do you think I felt when you abandoned me?"

"I'm asking you for the last time. Leave me in peace!" she moaned.

"Peace? *Il quieto vivere?* I wish to God I had peace in my life! If only you had believed me, I could have survived anything!" he said bitterly. "But no, you blanked out everything we'd been to one another, all knowledge of my feelings about honor and life and women, and descended into behaving like a petulant bitch who's been denied the dog she wants!"

She snatched breath from somewhere, her huge eyes dark with pain. Giovanni and Beth. Her lover and her best friend. That had been hard enough to take, seeing them together that night. Worse was seeing the two smashed cars and knowing that each contained someone she loved.

She put her hands over her ears, wishing she could shut out forever the sound of Beth screaming that awful night of the accident, hating the memory of the white-faced Giovanni shaking Beth violently and snarling at her to shut up before he reversed his car away from Sue's.

He had changed. There was no gentleness in him at all now. And she shuddered, wondering what two years in prison could do to an eighteen-year-old who'd loved his family and life with a wonderful zest and optimism. Every Christmas, each New Year, each Thanksgiving that she'd celebrated with her grandfather and Adriana, she'd wondered how Giovanni was coping, because he was so alone and no one was visiting him. Tears welled up to wash the blue eyes and she turned her head away.

"Prison . . . prison has brutalized you. . . ."

Her voice trailed away, choked by relentless emotions, and then his fingers were drawing her chin back, tilting it up so she was forced to meet his unreadable eyes. Emotions were taking their toll on him, too, perhaps the memories of the dark days in jail, and she winced in heartfelt sympathy. It was misplaced.

"*You* brutalized me," he accused harshly. A thumb scooped the tears from her cheeks without tenderness. And the sickness threatened to overwhelm her. Hastily she brought her hand to her mouth and swallowed back the hard lump in her throat. Giovanni's breath hissed in through his teeth, his merciless eyes flashing a spine-chilling warning that rooted her to the spot. "So you think you're suffering!" he mocked. "You don't even know you're born! But you will soon."

And she saw the raw anger in him, the sense of injustice he bore her as though he'd been brooding for all the intervening years and planning revenge. Nervously she looked around, hoping to catch the eye of a passerby and evade Giovanni, but the street was empty. In any case, she knew her only hope was to make him go. If he stayed for any length of time, even if there was a restraining order on him, he'd find out about Adriana.

Her heart lurched with sheer horror at the prospect. She *had* to shield Adriana from Giovanni, or he'd move heaven and earth to take her away. And the bewildered Adriana would scream and cry and he wouldn't give a damn.

A sense of tender protectiveness engulfed her at the horrible scenario. It must never happen. She'd make sure Giovanni left. Now.

Her head snapped up, her mouth tight with determination. "You're crazy to come here!" she said coldly. "You'll be recognized at any moment! Given half a chance, folks here'll tar and feather you!"

"And you?" he said, in a sinister tone.

"I'd be selling the brushes," she said curtly. "You really don't appreciate how strongly some folks feel. They have long memories."

"So do I," he said quietly, his eyes raking her body. And in the wake of his appraisal there came a sudden heat that radiated over her skin and made her suck in a breath sharply. "Memories that make me desire . . . action."

"Like what?" she asked huskily, and foolishly, before she knew it, she'd responded to the sudden dryness of her lips by licking them. She scowled, hoping to cover up her give-away reaction.

Giovanni smiled faintly but didn't answer the question. "You really think there's still bad feelings in Eternity about me?" he asked casually. "Even after all this time?"

"I know there is," she said in a low tone. *Go!* She pleaded with her eyes. *Go and leave us all alone!*

Unperturbed, he shifted his weight against the low parapet of the bridge and folded his arms confidently. "Bad feeling," he mused. "That's awkward."

"Why?" she asked warily.

"Because I'm coming back to live here," he replied with a pleasant smile, and walked off in the direction of her apartment while she stood staring at his retreating back in horror.

CHAPTER TWO

IT WAS A DREAM. A nightmare. But Tina saw the tall resolute figure in the cool cream suit turn to give her a mockingly seductive smile, and she knew from the hot spilling of hormones into her bloodstream that this was cold reality.

She could ignore the come-on and be safe. Walk away, get on with her day. Her finger slicked over the perspiration on her upper lip as she dismissed that choice.

Adriana's welfare came first. The last thing she wanted was for Giovanni to find out that she and her grandfather weren't alone anymore. Tina's heart thudded in alarm. If he was insensitive enough to hang around, he'd hear everything there was to know.

Adriana needed stability more than anything. Tina hoped she'd provided that. Love and attention, laughter and understanding had filled the small apartment, and she and her grandfather were devoted to Adriana. Without her, their lives would be less full, less rewarding. Tina let her eyes close, dreading the thought of losing her. They were family. Giovanni was an outsider, however closely he might be bound by blood to Adriana.

If he should assert his rights and demand access—or even custody—it would be unbearable. The days would be too empty. They'd gotten into the habit of washing one another's hair, curling up on the sofa with their eyes glued to some weepie on TV and trying out new recipes together.

What would Giovanni make of the trivial things that gave Adriana such pride? That neatly sewn apron, the final pompom on the knitted hat, the poem learned by heart.... *She* knew what milestones they were. Gio didn't. And Adriana would be hurt by his lack of praise and bewildered at being torn from her familiar, much-loved surroundings and the safe rituals.

Tina thought of her parents, devoting themselves to their teaching jobs in Puerto Rico, and how badly she missed her mother. Adriana had helped to fill that need for another female in the house who was close to her heart, someone to receive the huge amounts of love she needed to give to others.

But stupidly she'd forgotten Gio's rights. When she'd committed herself so completely to caring for Adriana, it had never crossed her mind that he'd come back to Eternity.

Her worried eyes focused on his striding figure. He was an inveterate liar. Perhaps his threat that he was intending to live in the town had been spite and nothing else. For Adriana, for her own peace of mind, she must make every effort to make sure he left Eternity before he talked to anyone.

Her body jerked into motion and she began to run, stumbling at first because her legs seemed to have lost their strength, and then finally catching up with him in a burst of fury and panic.

"Giovanni!" she panted, jogging along beside him while his long strides covered the ground rapidly. "You're bluffing, aren't you?" she asked anxiously. "You mean to drive off—"

"No." He glanced down at her briefly, a flash of triumph in his eyes. "I'm not."

"But why come here, of all places in the world?" she asked, a sense of dread settling in the pit of her stomach.

"For one thing," he said evenly, "I mean to persuade the folks around here to give me a different kind of character from the one you and your dear friend Beth landed me with."

"Beth?" She felt relieved that Beth was safely out of harm's way in Boston. But she was her ex-friend now. Giovanni's two-timing and the trial had killed their lifelong friendship stone dead. "How do you intend arranging that?" she asked with a worried frown.

"I have a very carefully thought-out plan," he said smoothly. "Time hangs heavily in jail. One has to do something to keep amused."

She flushed. "Gio, this is unrealistic. You *can't* come here to settle down! You're behaving like ... like a cartoon character!"

"Well, this is my fantasy and I'm making it happen," Giovanni said in mild sarcasm.

"Don't you have any concern for what I'd feel seeing you walking the streets? Or Grandpa?" she asked angrily.

"It's worth a little pain to get what you want," he said quietly.

Her shoulders drooped, her body slumping in distress, and she fell back a step or two. If he meant he wanted to give her pain, he was succeeding already. Grandpa would be hurt when he saw Gio, the man who'd killed his elder granddaughter and great-grandchild, driving around Eternity and showing no contrition, no sensitivity to their feelings. Then Adriana would be flung into the maelstrom....

Seeing Giovanni had forged on ahead again, Tina hurried to catch up. "If you stay," she reasoned, "you'll upset us—and Beth's parents, everyone who saw you that night, everyone who knew and loved Sue," she said passionately.

"Possibly."

Her mouth crimped with anger at his callousness. "Haven't you the decency to stay away? Didn't you learn anything from what happened?" she asked sadly.

"Yes," he replied. "Never to trust women." His beautiful, rich chocolate eyes were almost black with contempt, the long lush lashes spiking at her accusingly. "If you want to know what else I learned in prison, we'll need several hours and you'll need a strong stomach."

"Oh, Gio!" she whispered brokenly. She'd have done anything not to be driving him away. In her heart of hearts, if he'd been different—penitent, changed, less vengeful— she would have loved to see him with Adriana and would have gladly prepared the ground for them to accept one another. The wounds would have healed. But sadly, it seemed he was no fit guardian for her precious Adriana. "Gio, if only you'd come back to apologize..." she began wistfully. And hesitated. Perhaps there was hope. "You could. It would make everything quite different."

"I have nothing to apologize for," he said flatly. "You know, if you keep running along beside me, people will think you're chasing me. Amazing how people can get the wrong impression from an isolated event they witness, isn't it?"

Tina flushed at the implication, the quickly rising color making her feel even hotter than before. She eased her T-shirt from her sticky body under Giovanni's watchful dark eyes, then quickly smoothed her damp palms on her shorts and looked ahead as they strode on. Worryingly, a handful of students were still hanging around the derelict lot, discussing the car.

"I *did* see you in the driver's seat that night of the accident," she insisted. "You *did* hit my sister's car during a row with Beth, and all I want now is to watch you drive away before you hurt the people I love again!" she said miserably.

"Save your breath, Tina. You won't dissuade me from my intentions."

Suddenly he stopped, allowing his gaze to roam over her. And her soft-fringed eyes mistakenly lingered on him. Lisa had been right about the body language. He spoke fluent sensuality from every pore. Plenty of guys had spectacular muscles that left her cold, but Giovanni knew how to stand and move and project his masculinity and make a woman feel feminine and desirable and *hungry*. His sex appeal was earthy and direct and irresistible because he adored women and all that came with them.

Gorgeous, she thought hazily. He was absolutely gorgeous and totally evil. Incredibly she caught herself wishing she didn't look so scruffy and—

"Were you really so beautiful before?" he mused as if genuinely unsure. Her eyes must have shown the leap of surprised pleasure that had taken her unawares, because his mouth curved into a beguiling smile. "Tempting. Tantalizing. Mysterious."

"M-mysterious?" she stuttered, unable to help herself from asking.

"Then there's the distortion of time."

"Time?" She could have kicked herself for falling into his trap. The say-something-kooky trap, to get a woman interested. "Look—"

"It makes fools of us all," he said softly. "Because I can't recall that your eyes were such a deep blue. I could swear they're almost as clear as the lagoon. You know the way it sparkles and invites you to plunge right in." He gave her a disarming smile, but the words were enough to shake her.

Tina tried to muster some reply, a sharp crack perhaps, but his gaze had drifted to her mouth and she hesitated, wondering what lavish claims he'd make, all thought of coaxing him back to his car temporarily forgotten while she waited, quivering in anticipation.

"I remember that softness," he said huskily, his eyes caressing. "Know what they always reminded me of?" She shook her head wordlessly. "That silky texture of a petal. Poppies in the meadows," he mused with such a drowsy murmur that her mouth flowered into an even lusher pout of scarlet invitation. He smiled, breathing out hard so that his breath filtered tantalizingly over her lips till they parted. "I'm afraid that kissing you would tempt a man to linger too long for his safety."

Aware she was on the brink of sinking in shameful delight beneath the blatant flattery, she forced herself to remember that he was the last person she should allow to compliment her, a man convicted of manslaughter. Ex-convict. Ex-lover. *Ex! Ex!* she told herself fiercely.

"I said it wasn't healthy for you around here," she agreed huskily.

His mouth twitched. "You misunderstand. I'm staying. I've gone through too much to be scared off by townspeople," he said dismissively. He gave an enigmatic smile. "I have schemes to protect me from being tarred and feathered. Be patient. You'll learn about them soon enough."

Leaving her openmouthed in dismay, he made straight for her apartment door at the side of the garage, and before she could find her brains he'd put his finger on the bell and was keeping it there.

Tina slipped quickly through the picket gate to his side. "What are you doing?" she asked warily.

"Waiting."

She closed her eyes and offered up a brief thanks for deliverance. With her grandfather and Adriana on their way to Rockport—probably planning on exploring the delights of rock pools and the gift shops at Bearskin Neck, she thought fondly—she'd been saved an ugly scene.

"No one's in," she said.

"I'll hang around."

Alarmed, she ruthlessly calmed her nerves, wondering what he meant to do. Judging by the set of that smooth jaw, he had a purpose in mind and was going to see it through once his car was mended. But he was a mechanic! she thought, kicking herself for not remembering.

"If you can't handle the trouble with your car and can't wait for the part-timers," she suggested brightly, "try the garage in Ipswich. There's a pay phone nearby."

He smiled faintly, his cynical mouth curling at the corners. "There's nothing wrong with the car. I parked by the garage on purpose."

"Oh!" Stunned, she remembered the neat patch of oil, the handy car trolley and his still-immaculate suit. A setup. "What...purpose?" she said, her voice wavering, her nerves crumbling.

"I arranged the car—and myself," he said, ringing the bell impatiently again, "as a lure."

Her eyes widened. It had worked. "To bring me out?" she asked.

"Heaven forbid," he murmured, rolling eloquent eyes up to heaven. "I knew what *your* reaction would be when you saw me. I was hoping to lure out your grandfather."

"He's not about, and the garage is closed till the part-timers arrive," she said stiffly, still not understanding why he needed her grandfather. Her black eyebrows arched and disappeared beneath her bangs. "Have you run out of gas?"

"No. Patience," he answered dryly. "Where is Dan? He always started at seven."

"Not nowadays. He's nearly eighty," Tina reminded him shortly.

"I see. I thought he was probably still having breakfast. That's the reason I slid under the car to wait for him to come over and ask me what the trouble was." He smiled, his eyes distant as though remembering happier times. "He and I could smell out classic cars at a hundred paces. I was sure he'd be out like a shot."

"Seems an elaborate ploy," she said with a frown. "Why risk ruining your rented suit for that?"

A blankness deadened his eyes and he stared at her somberly for a while. "The stakes were high," he said eventually. "Worth a little subterfuge, a little waiting and some good honest dust."

Tina went cold. "Like I said, he's not in." Her tone was curt, her voluptuous mouth set in decidedly stubborn lines.

He looked upward, scanning the windows and frowning when he came to the small barred one. Tina held her breath. "I don't believe you. Let me in, Tina," he ordered.

Incredulous that he'd even consider asking, she said coldly, "Not on your life."

He leaned against the porch, elegant, cool and totally implacable. And his body language told her in no uncertain terms that he'd keep attempting to reach his declared goal and wouldn't let up. His arms were folded across the big chest, his legs were slightly spread, and his jaw stuck out ominously. She leaned against the opposite side, but for support, not display.

Languidly his hand reached out, and Tina's mesmerized eyes followed its progress to her throat. She swallowed, the flicker of his eyes telling her that he'd seen her fear. Then the tips of his fingers met her hot skin and she felt them slide over the slippery surface down to her collarbone.

"Nervous about something?" he murmured, lifting his fingers from her skin and holding out their sweat-dampened tips for her to explain.

"Hot. From running. You've got a long stride."

"I've got a long checklist to get through."

"Meaning?" she asked nervously.

The black velvet eyes glimmered. "I came to talk to your grandfather. Since he's not around, it seems I must make do with you, instead," he said in a lazy predatory drawl. "Alternatively, I could ask a few questions in town."

"What questions?" she asked, brazening it out.

"Anything there is to know about you, for a start. Since you're a school counselor, I imagine those students over there know a few things about you they'd be willing to divulge."

"Don't involve them!" she said quickly, hating to beg.

"Let me in and I won't need to."

She was silent. Her pulse throbbed heavily in her temples, and she put her fingers there for relief so she could think straight. It was the uncertainty she couldn't stand. There were three possibilities: either he knew about Adriana, or he suspected something, or he knew nothing at all. But if she invited him in to talk sense into him, he'd see enough evidence to give the game away after a few minutes.

"You can't come up," she said firmly. "People will talk."

"Plan C, then." With a casual shrug, he strolled over to his car. Tina waited, holding her breath. A bluff. He'd get in the car and drive away....

He began talking to Lisa. She fumed as Lisa and Giovanni laughed together, his sun-shot blond head bent low over hers. Recognizing that look of admiration Lisa was giving him, Tina winced. If she didn't move soon, he'd dispense with the preliminaries and ask a few direct incriminating questions.

Angrily she stomped across the lot to where Giovanni was holding court.

"Oh, yes, known her for years," he was saying. The students stared at Tina in awe as she came closer, and he smiled at her in a sickeningly winsome way. "We've been talking over old times," he said in a husky reminiscing tone of voice. "You know the kind of thing. The high school prom, the homecoming dance, old films, clambakes."

Tina eyed him cynically. "Time you went home, Gio. Byee!"

"It was at a clambake," he remarked idly to his rapt audience, ignoring her completely, "that Tina poured a half-gallon tub of melted chocolate ice cream—"

"Please!" she protested indignantly.

"—into the school bully's gas tank," he finished.

Four pairs of astonished eyes turned on Tina's flushed face.

"You'll give them ideas, Gio," she muttered.

"I could," he said worryingly. "Shall we continue our chat indoors, Teen? I'm ready if you are," he added with an encouraging lift of his eyebrow.

She screwed her mouth up tightly at his misuse of her name. "I'm heading for the beach in a while." Somehow she dug up a smile for the students' benefit. "Aren't you all off to the beach, too?" she suggested to them hopefully.

Giovanni grinned amiably at the fascinated group. "Or you guys could take a moment to sit in the car, try it for size. Feel free."

There was a chorus of enthusiastic agreement, so he obligingly opened the Lamborghini's passenger-side door. Watching the excited faces, hearing him answering the eager queries, she grudgingly admired the way he had won the interest of the students. He'd done something for them; now it would be their turn to do something for him. Like answering his questions, she thought with apprehension.

And their eyes met, his triumph plain to see. Tina felt trapped, wanting to run away but unable to. It seemed that whatever she did, he'd find out that she'd kept a secret from him all these years. One so important that by rights she should have told him.

"I won't be long, darling," he said warmly to Tina. At her gasp, he gave a theatrical groan and a sheepish grin, releasing appealing laughter lines around his dark eyes. "I've let the cat out of the bag!" he exclaimed. "I suppose they don't even know we were once close friends—"

"Stop it, Gio!" Tina interrupted desperately.

"Aw, shucks! Mustn't tease my best girl, must I?" He grinned, grabbing her around the waist and pulling her fondly into his hip. He looked down at her as if they were lovers reunited.

Tina wanted to hit him. Aw, shucks and best girl indeed! She caught the look in Giovanni's eye and was furious to see that he was vastly amused by the way he'd put her on the defensive. Time she got Giovanni somewhere he couldn't bring her name into disrepute! Already his hipbone was burning into hers with more heat than friends ought to generate between them.

"Not if you want to reach thirty, you mustn't," Tina agreed lightly, without a clue in the world as to how to get rid of him safely. But at least she could lose their audience while she did it. So she swallowed her pride and her fear, flashed him a big friendly smile and tucked her arm in his. "I might see you guys at the beach," she said to the students. "If I'm carrying a tub of ice cream, it's because I'm going to take my revenge on a bully—"

"I hope you're not planning on pouring it into my gas tank," he said with a low laugh, squeezing her waist with his big crushing hand and making her gasp.

"No," she said sweetly. "Down your cream suit."

He chucked her indulgently under the chin. "Saucy witch!" he said fondly. His lips parted and his eyes became drugged with a drowsy desire. "You know I'd make you lick it off."

There was an intake of breath all round. Giovanni's trick of wrapping each word in curling sensuality had made that sound like a highly erotic act. Red in the face with embarrassment, Tina felt his fingers sliding down her hip, and she could see from the expression on the students' faces that she needed to play the remark down or she'd lose all credibility as an upholder of the moral tone.

"Idiot," she said fondly. "Don't take any notice of this guy," she said in an offhand way to the students, trying to hold his roaming hand still. The rhythm was penetrating her bones and creating far-reaching vibrations in places she'd rather not remember. "He's a real joker. Won the debating prize most years. You know the kind. All talk, no do. Come on," she said, grimly shooting the amused Giovanni a hands-off look. "Tell your aunty Teen what you've been up to since you left and how your lovely wife is and your—is it eight?—children. Loves kids," she confided, her voice a little wobbly now from the strain. "Bye, everyone. Have a nice day."

With knowing smirks that made her want to scream, the teenagers wandered away and Tina drew in a deep breath. First blow to her. And then her brief sense of deliverance vanished rather rapidly when she found herself being firmly propelled toward her apartment door.

"I knew you'd see sense," murmured Giovanni.

"Now it's your turn," began Tina. But suddenly she found his arms around her. "Gio!" she warned huskily.

"Mmm?" he said with a slow smile.

She felt his long fingers sliding down her back and tensed, ready to raise her knee and... Tina blinked rapidly. Both his hands were pushed into the side pockets of her shorts, and for a few delicious seconds her hipbones were being treated to a seductive massage. She stiffened, motionless as a statue. Giovanni's long fingers had crept into the warm socket beyond her pelvic bones and the caress was driving heat into her loins. Lovely liquid heat that made her back arch involuntarily and her head lift till her face was uptilted and available.

He murmured something and then laughed softly. She heard a clink and saw that he was waving her key in front of her nose.

"No!" she wailed, furious with herself for not realizing what he was doing. *Always* he tricked her. *Always* she fell for it! Angrily she shot her hand up for the key. He lifted it higher, waggling it about in smug triumph. Tall he might be, but she could jump, couldn't she? And wipe that smile off! Her knees flexed and she sprang into the air just as he stepped closer. And to anyone watching, it must have seemed she'd leapt into his waiting embrace with unseemly eagerness.

Giovanni reacted with typical enthusiasm. "Tina!" he said silkily, wrapping his arms around her with the speed of lightning.

Helplessly she kicked her dangling legs in midair only too uncomfortably aware that her body was being pressed into his and her mouth had ended up inches away from his jaw. "Opportunist!" she gasped, the breath being crushed from her. To her horror, she saw a movement at the Alden place and her eyes widened in dismay. "Put me down!" she yelped.

He glanced behind him and also saw that Lisa had returned and was straightening up from collecting something she'd left behind by the car. With a cruelly mocking grin, he turned back, at the same time casually kicking out at a gas can stowed in the porch.

"I think you'd better stop wiggling," he said huskily. "I'm enjoying it too much. Do you *know* where your pelvis is?"

The distraught Tina went instantly limp. Of course she knew! Wasn't she wishing she didn't? "Put me down!" she whispered, her mouth a lick away from his. "Lisa must have heard the rattle of the can...."

"Oh, do you think so?" he asked innocently. "I imagine she's glancing over now, don't you? I'm afraid," he added gravely, "that it'll look as if we're locked in a friendly clinch."

"Manipulator! Down!" she whispered fiercely against his laughing mouth.

"If you insist. Mmm. Gorgeous." His mouth drifted lower to her throat. A hand, thrust between them, crept to the top of her thighs.

"I...mmm! I meant *down* as in put me down!" she mumbled breathily, feeling the quick rush of flowing need spreading from where his hand had briefly rested and radiating through her whole body.

"Okay."

One arm alone held her slight weight. She heard the sound of the key being inserted into the lock, but before she could protest, she was being carried inside and the door had slammed. Almost immediately Giovanni let her go and she tumbled to the floor in the hallway at the bottom of the stairs. So did he.

"Well, this is nice," he murmured, halfheartedly untangling his legs from hers. "Like Bambi and Thumper, when they bumped on the ice." She gave him a look of loathing, and his hand clamped around her chin. Her mutinous eyes glowered at him, he gave her a crooked grin, then touched his lips to hers.

"*They* were friends," she muttered through the kiss, unwillingly adoring the taste of him as her inner lip moved against his mouth.

"I love your sulky pout. Mmm. Your tongue's so sour tipped when you talk to me and yet you're really tasty," he mused. "Must be all those doughnuts. Sugar sweet. I'm crazy about sweet things. Chocolate ice cream on naked flesh, honey-tipped breasts, your luscious poppy red lips. Come here."

"Gio!" she protested, deeply shocked. His mouth swooped on hers again and she felt his laugh shape the kiss and his breath feeding into her with a rush of deliciously tingling warmth. Weakly she fought the instant pleasure, appalled that she found it wonderful to be drowning in his arms once more and that it was a joy to be mingling the taste of her lips with his, inhaling the clean-showered scent of his body and experiencing the feeling of satin stroking satin as his mouth explored hers.

Sun warm, his mouth, she thought dazedly, pushing at his shoulders because she knew she must. Kisses deep and driving and dangerous. Thoroughly wanton. A hand crawled up her back, and she arched away when all her instincts told her to wriggle into the sweep of his palm and let him explore every curve of her warm body.

With a sudden effort she broke free, her mouth strangely reluctant to do anything more than hold its crushed-kiss pout. Feeling sick with herself, she took a huge breath and said, "Get out!"

"Sure. When I'm satisfied," he replied in a sexy growl.

Her eyes widened in alarm. She was alone. With a guy who couldn't control himself. God, her sex drive had driven her mad! "Giovanni!" she whispered shakily. "You...you wouldn't..." Fear cut off her vocal cords. He was gently stroking the shimmering skin that stretched over her collarbone, a look of dangerous lust in his eyes as he gazed at her.

"I will do whatever I have to," he said softly.

His body shifted a little closer. She felt the warmth of him a breath or two away and her lips parted in a whimper. The blond head lowered, offering her the full impact of its glorious sun-bleached curls, tousled charmingly by the fall, cascading in touchable damp tendrils on his smoothly tanned forehead. Two dark eyes melted into hers.

A spear of something unrecognizable caught her unawares and made her quiver from head to foot. Her head spun. Flu, she thought. A stomach bug. Just when she needed all her strength.

And then she was swallowing back a cry of alarm because his powerful arms and body were forming an imprisoning cage around her, and she knew that if she attempted to come upright, she couldn't avoid being pressed intimately against him again. The thought made her feel sick. That strong male body. The hard muscular thighs...

A sudden flash of sexual reaction ripped through her, from loins to stomach, to breasts, throat and mouth, her lips flowering into an unwilling lushness. It wasn't sickness, she thought, appalled. It was a totally unwelcome carnal excitement that had overtaken her and refused to go away.

My sister is dead, she said to herself. *Her child is dead. Gio killed them.* The destructive desire receded a little. To her eternal shame, it ebbed away more slowly than it had come.

He smiled mockingly as if he knew everything that was going on inside her and growled with sexy appreciation in his golden throat. "So it still happens," he marveled. "You become aroused by a look, a gesture, by the passing of warm breath over your ultrasensitive skin." He gazed at her through the dark fringe of lashes, his expression infinitely seductive. "I do so love the combination of madonna and whore in your makeup."

"That's insulting!" she cried with hot-faced indignation. "Being near you makes me sick with disgust!"

"Sure?"

His knowing eyes played on her trembling body in a slow and devastatingly sexy prelude to possession, and to her utter dismay she felt each part tense painfully in turn and leave a tingle on the skin that seeped deeper into each receptive pore. Although he was caressing her only with his eyes, it was as though he was lightly drawing his fingers across her body in a sensual movement that snaked thrillingly down her throat and across her naked shoulders. She *was* sick with something—hunger, emptiness, a lost dream.

Pain flashed through her, the pain of misery and violent need. The shock of her response thickened her tongue, and it was a great effort to say what she had to. "I'm sure," she rasped, even those two words wavering.

"I don't think you're sure at all. Your big blue eyes are a real giveaway," he said with a contemptuous drawl. His voice became husky. "They're glazed and they're alarmed and they're begging."

"No!" she denied, making them as narrow as she could.

He smiled mockingly. "And your beautiful mouth is asking to be kissed so prettily," he said, touching her hot swollen lower lip. His finger traced a delicate trail to the corner, and it was all she could do to keep her mouth closed and not groan in hunger. "Then there's your breathing," he murmured.

"My...what?" she said jerkily, and blinked. She'd squeaked, actually squeaked! Her obvious horror at her own self-betrayal made him smile triumphantly.

"Very shallow, rapid, rather rasping," he observed with a solicitous smile. "Health problem or me?"

Bodies were treacherous, she thought irritably. They had long memories. She suffered a cruel split-second reminder of their exciting union—wild, passionate, utterly satisfying and perfectly wonderful to her innocent mind and body. Pushing away the memory of his golden body above hers in all its naked glory, she squirmed beneath his knowing stare and tried to concentrate.

"Anger!" she explained in a furious croak.

His eyebrow lifted cynically. "Uh-huh."

"It *is*," she muttered, incensed that he was able to invest such depth of meaning in one little "uh-huh."

"I'd advise you not to get angry too often, then," he said. "The results do the most alarming things to your lovely breasts and only a saint would keep his hands off them. In case you hadn't noticed," he added unnecessarily, "I'm not a saint."

She folded her arms with difficulty. There seemed to be a lot of her in the way suddenly. "Keep your eyes and your mind off my body!" she mumbled. "And get in your dream machine and drive off into the blue yonder!" she added in despair.

"I would if I could, believe me," he said, spreading his hands in a gesture of helplessness. "But I have too many memories of your eager responses. Like when I was dating Beth and had dropped her off with her aunt. You and I were stuck in my car while the blizzard raged around us...."

Tina bristled. "I was cold. You said you'd warm me up. You were the one coming on to *me*," she said tightly.

A faint smile tilted the corners of his expressive mouth, and Tina found herself staring at it, hopelessly remembering his first gentle respectful kiss. "I think you were with me every step of the way," he said quietly.

"I was scared," she countered, ruthlessly obliterating the dreamlike quality of the kiss and her naively delighted demands for more. He'd obliged, of course. Till she was dizzy and intoxicated with love. "I needed comfort. I was afraid we'd be stranded," she explained.

"No, you weren't. You hoped we might be," he reminded her brutally.

She lifted a stubborn chin. "Only because I wanted to miss study period."

Giovanni laughed, his even teeth dazzling white in his dark handsome face. Tina felt her heart lurch infuriatingly as it used to in the days when she'd been shamelessly and helplessly in love with her best friend's lover. Being kissed by him in the car had been her secret dream come true. Other than Brent Powell, who'd been Giovanni's rival in every walk of life, Gio was the most desirable guy in school.

Brent was everything a mother would want for her daughter. Giovanni had an edge of danger, a rawness that made him exciting. Mothers didn't want him for their daughters; they wanted him for themselves.

"You're deluding yourself," he said in amusement. "You were nuts about me."

"I was nuts, all right," she muttered. "You were a fake charmer. You fooled us all."

"But not anymore?" His eyes grew soft with warm melting desire and his fingers lightly brushed her bare arm. "God!" he breathed huskily. "You look sinfully wanton and inviting sprawled out like that!"

Fear killed the initial flame of pleasure that lit her up inside. She edged backward, feeling the hard line of the stairs against her spine. Giovanni didn't move, but she could see his muscles were tensed, ready, his eyes working over her body as though she were in a shop window or a cheap peep show.

Against her rib cage, her heart beat frantically, and try as she might, she couldn't stop the fear from welling up inside. "Don't touch me!" she whispered.

He caught her in his strong grip, and she froze as he boldly slid one hand under her T-shirt to cup her breast. "But I have to," he said softly. "There are things my body and soul cry out for. Things I need, or I can't be content. Don't you see?" And his mouth descended ruthlessly on hers.

Tina couldn't even struggle. Weeping inside in frustrated anger, she gritted her teeth to steel herself against the slow, torturing rhythm of the finger and thumb that delicately rubbed the already throbbing peak of her breast, whisking it shockingly to harder and tighter tension and thus arousing every inch of her love-starved body with a perfectly timed, accurately judged pressure. Enough to drive her wild. Enough to make her lean in to him for more. Enough of a kiss to divert her attention, enough to remind her....

"Mmm..." she moaned.

He became still, his hands wandering to her waist while she strained against him hungrily for more. A terrible anger filled her. He was going to cheat her body of its needs. Slowly his mouth lifted from hers and his dark unfathomable eyes fixed her with a tenacious stare. "Is that a capitulation?" he murmured huskily.

"I'll..." She fought for breath, for some composure and for time.

"Give in, Tina!" he commanded softly. "You know how it is between us. There's never been anyone as good, has there?"

It was the slightly hesitant query that alerted her. Lifting her lashes briefly to identify the cause, she saw with a firing spurt of satisfaction that he wasn't quite as indifferent as he pretended. His breathing was ragged, his chest rose and fell with jerky irregularity, and he looked more than a little glazed. He did desire her. He wanted confirmation that he was the greatest lover on God's earth—and that meant she had a potential weapon.

Giovanni Kowalski cared only for bodily pleasures, and his desire was nothing more than an animal urge. He was man. She was woman. Prison had changed him and made his nature even more carnal than before.

Yet it meant that she had *something* she could bargain with. Since he wanted her, maybe she could stop him from going upstairs, from seeing the evidence that pointed to Adriana's presence. She scowled. Except she'd have to only *pretend* she'd fallen for his seduction. Whatever she did, she was wedged between a rock and a hard place.

Her instinct was to protect the vulnerable Adriana and shield her from all knowledge of Giovanni's visit. *And* to keep Giovanni at arm's length. *And* to abandon all sense and slither into his waiting arms! Was she confused?

"You're rushing me," she said huskily, stalling for time, contemplating a suggestion of a drive in the Lamborghini. Did that make her a temptress? Would she deserve scorn for leading him on? And if he agreed, what she'd do then she couldn't imagine. Struggle in the back seat, probably. "I need a bit of time...."

"Forget the convention of waiting," he added roughly. "We've been down that road before. You want me and I want you. Here's the proof."

Lazily he lifted her limp, despairingly unresisting hands above her head. She knew she must protest, but her brain wouldn't accept the slow message. Seconds passed and it was too late. He'd lowered his body to hers, the whole warm glorious length of him balanced with just the right amount of force bearing down on her. She groaned and lost her protest in the pleasure of his searching kiss.

"I think this is the moment to go upstairs and explore," he murmured seductively in her ear.

"No!" she croaked. That was the last thing she wanted! "Not upstairs...here! No, I mean..." She turned a confused and pinkened face to his. "Gio, we can't! Not here."

"Make up your mind," he drawled lazily. "Afraid someone will come back and surprise us frolicking on the doormat?"

She felt the heat of his loins rising, the hardness of his body unnervingly virile and excitingly urgent. "Yes!" she cried in an outrush of breath.

"So your grandfather's coming back."

"No. Yes! No! Not for two weeks!" she gasped, as Giovanni sighed and curved his big hands around her breasts. "I mean...please..." Her body arched beneath him.

"I will, once we establish *where,*" he murmured, his fingers taking an intense delight in her silken warmth.

"The...the beach," she said breathlessly, trying to twist away. "I'll get...the picnic. We'll...go for a s-swim and..."

Tina felt her eyes closing and her body relaxing, giving in to hedonistic pleasure. Giovanni was kissing her naked breasts with total concentration, his lashes thick on his golden cheekbones, and he was the most beautiful thing she'd ever seen and what he was doing was producing the most beautiful sensation in the world. And she was out of her mind.

"Gio," she gasped. "Don't..." Her body seemed to be flowing all over the floor and her brain couldn't sort out the right messages. All she kept getting was desperate signals from the most intimate parts of her body that they wanted Giovanni's touch, for him to kiss and caress her till dark, and then some more.

CHAPTER THREE

"So, Tina," he said thickly, one finger lightly massaging her embarrassingly hard nipple, "what's it to be? You choose. A roll in the hay, a furtive tumble in the dunes...or will you tell me where my mother is?"

She froze. "Your...mother?" she repeated stupidly.

He dipped his head to the wet peaks and lapped at them like a satisfied cat, watching them jerk spasmodically. "Mmm. I...went to...her house...." he said slowly, then cleared his throat. "She's not there." His lashes flicked up suddenly, seeing the alarm in her enormous blue eyes.

"No, she left," she said, hardly recognizing her own voice in the thick labored sounds.

His expression became cynical. "So I gather from the old lady who lives there now. Mother left years ago. Nice for me to know."

Tina met his cold bleak eyes and felt a great sadness that he'd lost touch with his mother. And even sadder at the cause. "You knew she'd disowned you," she said quietly.

There was a quick glitter in the dead eyes. "Yes. However, I did at least expect to be kept informed of her address," he said harshly. "The old lady didn't have it, but your grandfather will. He and my father were good friends. That's why I came to see him. Since he's away, you're going to tell me—or find out pretty damn quick."

His eyes glittered with a metallic light that scared her. Slowly he pulled her defenseless body to a sitting position, holding her fast. His high Slavic cheekbones looked more pronounced than usual. The brooding intensity he'd inherited from his Polish father had never been more apparent.

He had his father's fiery temper, his mother's sense of Sicilian justice. And that meant trouble, she thought, wary of Giovanni's explosive nature.

He'd gotten into a rage with Beth when she'd refused both his advances and his plea for her father's assistance in financing a place at Harvard. In a blind fury, he'd jammed his foot on the accelerator and driven straight into Sue's car. He'd sworn Beth had been driving, even though there were enough eyewitnesses to call him a liar. And she had been one of them. His anger had awed them all.

Tina trembled, her gaze colliding with his. Time, apparently hadn't lessened his sense of betrayal. It had deepened it. Transfixed by his cold stare, she swallowed, trying to get rid of the awful lump blocking her throat.

Mustering up courage and contempt, she said, "I refuse to be threatened. Is that what this is all about? You're trying to find your mother?"

"Why else would I come over from Sicily?" he replied huskily, a raw emotion in his tone that made her eyes glisten with sad tears.

Sicily! He must have gone there when he'd left jail, back to his mother's family, the country where he'd been born, to lick his wounds. Praying he'd go right back, she said unevenly, "I'm sorry. You've had a wasted journey. I understand she's gone away."

"Where?" he demanded urgently.

Defiantly, holding back her sorrow, she lifted her chin. "Why would I know?"

"Why, indeed." He released her, his face stark with disappointment.

"Gio," she mumbled compassionately.

He pulled her to her feet and stepped back, opening the apartment door. "You were going to the café," he said noncommittally.

Half blinded by tears, she nodded and stepped out into the brilliant sunshine. Giovanni strode toward his car, and with every stride she felt her heart tearing, strand by strand, till it seemed there was nothing left, no heavy beat, only the stillness of the aftermath of a storm.

She'd done it. He was leaving and— Oh, God! she groaned. She needed to be alone, to walk, to swim... Any physical exercise would do to take her mind from Giovanni and the dark days that had returned to haunt her.

Without another thought in her head, she ran to the café, her mind still on hold. But standing at the counter, staring at the menu on the blackboard, she felt that she didn't want to eat at all because she felt so chewed up inside.

"Teen, Teen! You okay?"

"Oh, yes. Dreaming," she said hastily, seeing Teresa Silva's concerned eyes on her. "Nightmares. College placements," she explained with a roll of her eyes to the ceiling. "Gruesome workload."

"You work too hard. Take a break today—it's going to be a scorcher. Manuel's going crazy, keeping everything fresh for the weddings today." She smiled, as she always did when she spoke of her son, and Tina smiled back.

"I thought he'd be busy with the catering," Tina said. "Grandpa's left endless lists for our part-timers so that the limos are polished to exhaustion."

"We're all glad of the business." Teresa grinned. "What'll you have? The tuna melt's good, or I can do you a gilded lily...."

"Oh, tuna melt and pineapple muffins to go. And I'll pick out some fruit," Tina answered, trying to sound cheerful. Trying to *be* cheerful.

Yet once outside the diner, the tears began to fall again onto the back of her hand, and she knuckled her eyes irritably when she heard the door open behind her and someone came out.

"Teen, something *is* wrong," came Teresa's gentle voice in her ear. "Is it Adriana? Is she getting too much for you, what with your job and everything?"

"No." She sniffed. "I can manage. You know I love her."

"It can't be easy. I suppose you couldn't afford more help?"

"No," said Tina gloomily. Soon even the part-time help from Lal, a local retired nurse, would be out of the question. "We'll manage," she said optimistically, thinking of the joy that Adriana brought to them. "I can always take a summer job. Juggling—I'm good at that," she said with a grin.

"You're a saint," crooned Teresa, hugging Tina's slender shoulders warmly.

"Saints don't mope, they spread sunshine and light." Tina smiled wryly through her tears. Her head lifted. She needed sunshine and light. Time to herself, time to be alone, time to think and recover her bounce again. Adriana was safely out of town and Giovanni had gone, anyway. If she didn't get some space, she'd go mad. "I'm going to the beach to lie in the sun and do nothing but blink and breathe and walk and swim," she said in determination, wiping away all the evidence of her tears.

"Go for it." Teresa chuckled. "Enjoy."

Her expectations were that she'd do just that. Between Eternity and the sea flowed the Sussex River and a meandering tributary. Fishermen drifted around in small boats, it was often possible for lovers to be alone, to laze in a small boat with the sun on their skin, talking, sharing dreams. Dreams of love. Giovanni.

Feeling wistful, Tina returned to her apartment and collected everything she needed for the day, then drove out of town. The houses petered out to reveal the low glacial hills between which were marshes and cranberry bogs. She breathed in the fresh clean air with its tang of salt and began to calm down.

Tired from working flat out, emotionally drained by some of the problems she'd had to deal with, she often came to this natural wilderness, sometimes with Adriana but usually alone. And her mind would be restored to its usual optimism and joy by the mere act of watching the birds of the wetlands—the herons, the grebes and the exotic white egrets.

The breeze from the Atlantic would blow through her hair, she'd smell the salt of the marshlands and the rich

how much they had in common. She wished she'd never let him know that she worshiped him.

He'd dated her and dated Beth, too, lying to them both, swearing undying love to each of them. Beth, her longtime friend, who'd taken her under her wing, the rich, glamorous and dazzlingly beautiful Beth, who'd lived in the huge Tamblyn mansion by the wharf and had servants, orchards, a boathouse, a garden to envy and a four-stall garage.

Amazingly Beth had loved Tina's poky apartment, declaring it warm and cozy and full of laughter, instead of big and drafty and empty. Tina hadn't understood that. The Tamblyn house was the most beautiful property in Eternity, built by a Cornishman, Azariah Tamblyn, in the nineteenth century, and she would have been overjoyed to live in the mansion of a bewhiskered sea captain who'd made his fortune in the China trade. Though she did feel it was a house without love.

Beth seemed to find all the love she needed with the Murphy family. And with lavish generosity, Beth had given Tina clothes, teaching her how to play down her too-voluptuous figure. In exchange, Tina had helped Beth with her homework, loyally defended the criticisms and rumors about Beth's vindictive nature, and listened to her stories about the guys who were madly in love with her....

Especially the sexy new arrival, Giovanni, who apparently couldn't keep his hands off the cool, reserved and definitely hard-to-get Beth. Lying on her bed, with Beth acting out every meeting, every exciting proposition, Tina had watched wide-eyed and increasingly breathless as Beth showed her where and how Giovanni had tried to touch her.

"Horny," Beth had said dismissively. She spoke of sex like it was something dirty, and Tina had tried not to reveal her burgeoning interest because nice girls weren't supposed to like physical excess. "He's as frustrated as hell—wild and greedy," Beth had confided. "And he's rather rough."

So Tina had continued to learn about the pantingly eager Giovanni and to hide her own feelings for him, because

he was so obviously crazy about the ice-maiden Beth and
wouldn't look twice at a hotheaded Irish-American without an ounce of blue blood in her. He was clever and ambitious. Marriage to someone rich and influential would
help him achieve his goals.

But when—after the time of the blizzard—he'd asked
Tina for a date, telling her he and Beth were finished, she'd
been glad to believe the lie. Joyously, recklessly, she'd exchanged years of friendship for the chance to be in Giovanni's arms.

Inevitably his lies caught up with him. Beth read him the
riot act. He'd lost his cool and they'd argued. Seeing the
collapse of all his plans to persuade Beth's father to spon-
sor his college education, he'd gone berserk—with disas-
trous results.

It was that simple. Tina had to accept that she was partly
responsible for the chain of events that had led up to that
moment, and she felt intensely ashamed that she'd made
such a bad mistake in an otherwise blameless life.

Her grandfather thought she was a perfect little gem. Her
parents were proud of her. She was highly regarded in the
high school by students and staff alike. Little Miss Wonderful. But she'd betrayed the trust of her best friend, and
a long friendship had withered and died in acrimony, torn
to shreds by Beth's testimony and that of her parents, who'd
been key witnesses to the fatal accident from a window of
the Tamblyn house itself.

A door banged as someone came into the change house,
and Tina jumped up, startled. In doing so, she looked down
at herself and stopped in dismay. She imagined his eyes on
the provocatively high-cut legs of her suit, the thinness of
the material over her hips and loins that left nothing to an
imagination as fertile as Gio's....

Her hands stilled. Too much cleavage! she thought in
panic. Too much of her all-round. Each breast was lovingly cradled by the fine lycra, each globe proudly outlined
as if she was advertising them for general consumption!

But there wasn't much she could do about it now, short of staying in the change house till dark. Her mouth curved into a wry smile. She was darned if she was missing out on a day at the beach because of Gio's preoccupation with sex!

Mutinously she stuffed her clothes into the locker and carefully avoided looking at herself in the long mirror till she'd placed her beach towel decorously in front of her body and sneaked a glance to see the effect. Her laughter echoed through the building. She looked like someone in a nudist film hiding their essentials.

"To hell with it," she muttered. Rolling the towel up, she stalked proudly out of the change house and into the blinding sunshine, almost falling over Giovanni, who was waiting outside.

"Santa Maria!" he exclaimed. "Never had high school guidance counselors like that in my day," he murmured as she passed, nose in the air, with a little wiggle of her fingers in Cathy's direction.

"Miss Murphy's wonderful," Cathy said warmly.

"I know. I know that *very* well," agreed Giovanni silkily.

Tina's back stiffened and she heard his soft laugh, but no more once she reached the boardwalk that led to the beach. She desperately hoped that Cathy's imminent exam would take priority over answering any of Giovanni's questions.

But she couldn't take that chance. So when she reached the top of the dune she turned and gave him a long slow look over her shoulder. Then made a solemn promise to herself. *I will enjoy this day. This is my day. Gio won't—can't spoil it.*

Feeling better, fiercer, she eagerly ran down the steps onto the dazzling white beach, taking her sandals off immediately so that she could enjoy the sensation of her bare feet sinking into the soft, almost too-hot-to-touch sand. Hedonistically she wriggled each foot as she walked, letting the grains sift through her brown toes. Then she stopped to close her eyes in bliss and soak up the sun on her upturned face.

"Beautiful."

She didn't turn at the sound of his voice but stood staring out to the dazzling sea, pretending the huskily murmured word had no effect on her at all. And as if he didn't exist, she began to walk on again till she'd reached the flat firm sands. The sun beat down like a hammer striking an anvil, reflecting off the brilliant sea. Already she could feel her exposed skin starting to burn, and she dropped her towel and bag near a woman with a small baby.

He was still in his business suit. There was one place she could escape him, she thought in glee, and ran like crazy into the welcoming water.

Its iciness made her gasp, but she plunged on and soon the water felt cool and silky around her hot body, swirling around and over her like a lover's hands.

She frowned at where her mind had taken her and stole a glance at the beach. A distant cream-clad figure sat by her bag. Which contained her lunch. And she was starving! Crossly she swam for a long while, but the pangs of hunger didn't ease up. She had no choice but to face him again.

At least the worst had been said, the unpleasant things had been touched upon. On this occasion, she vowed, Giovanni wouldn't disturb her equilibrium.

By the time she'd reached the shallows, he was there beside her, his pants rolled up to the knees. He was holding out her towel for her like some solicitous butler tending to his master. He should have looked ridiculous, but he didn't. Instead, he seemed tender and caring, and she wanted to snuggle into the towel and let him cuddle her dry.

"Okay, Jeeves," she said crisply, snatching the towel from his overenthusiastic hands as they began to help dry her body. "I can do that myself, if you don't mind."

"Out of your depth?" he inquired wickedly.

"In this?" Calmly she kicked upward with her foot, showering them both with water, delighted in his instinctive flinch as the spray half drenched him. "I've been in deeper water," she said casually.

"Not half as deep as where you're heading," he murmured with soft savagery. She shivered, feeling suddenly cold. Then as he reached out to her, she stumbled, and they were both lying full-length in the shallows, Giovanni's body looming menacingly over hers as she struggled to get her breath and the waves kept throwing the Atlantic in her face.

"Help me up!" she yelled, swallowing salt water and choking.

"You're in no danger from the sea." Laughing, his face streaming with water, he retrieved his sunglasses, then hauled her up, the sea streaming from her in a silver cascade. She wasn't too pleased with his order of priorities. His hair was plastered to his head and shedding water on her upturned face like icy rain. "Perhaps you are from me," he murmured in her ear, steadying her as the rollers sought to push them through the sandy shallows.

Still trying to recover her breath, Tina cowered as his glistening bronze face came closer. "You've soaked your rented suit!" she said with some satisfaction.

"Oh, that's not important. It's worth it for the pleasure I'm getting," he said mockingly, and lifted her helpless body till it touched his.

Then just when she thought his softly parted lips would finish the punishment by claiming hers, he picked her up bodily and strode through the glittering golden water, his strong legs pushing through the frothing waves as though they didn't exist, while she lay exhausted and demoralized in his arms, wishing she'd remembered that only an idiot with a death wish ever tried to make a Sicilian look a fool.

"Are you all right?" It was such a considerately spoken question and his expression was so concerned that she found herself nodding. His hand caressed her face, and immediately she felt a tingle of energy as if they'd made an electric circuit. "The sun will warm you soon," he soothed.

"I can walk now," she muttered rebelliously. "Walking will warm me up."

He allowed her to slide to the ground, her body slithering deliciously through his wet hands. "Running would be even better," he suggested.

"I'm too tired."

"I imagine your work takes a lot out of you," he said quietly.

Slanting suspicious eyes at him, she accepted his offered hand after a moment's hesitation. There was no point in staggering on without help when he'd caused her predicament. Their heels sank into the soft, almost muddy sand near the water's edge in a way that Tina had always found sensuous.

"Yes, it does. It's draining," she said, mollified by his question. "But I love it. I live, eat and breathe my job."

"Nothing better to do?" he probed.

"It's that kind of a job," she replied huffily. "You have to pitch in with your whole heart. It's not just admin and courses, Gio. I deal with emotional and study problems, as well. I get to know my students and to care for them—and I protect them from trouble and troublemakers, so don't go taking their minds off their work," she said in warning.

"I suppose I could be a bit of a distraction if I tried," he agreed.

It was a deliberate taunt and gave a clue as to where his questions had been leading. He wasn't interested in her job at all! Hurt, Tina stopped and whirled around to face him, whisking water everywhere like a spaniel shaking itself.

"You let your roving eye pause on any one of them for longer than a nanosecond and you won't know what hit you!" she declared hotly.

"I love your hair in wet tendrils," he mused.

"Yours will be in chunks on the ground if you don't promise never to play Casanova with the women around here!" she retorted.

"I was thinking of playing Casanova with one woman in particular," he said innocently.

"Who?" she asked warily.

"You." He smiled, and Tina saw herself reflected in the black, salt-splattered lenses of his sunglasses; wet and tangle-haired, pouting and wide-eyed—and curving in far too many places for decency. "You see," he continued, flicking water from his forehead, "above everything, I want to be reunited with my mother, and I have a way of making sure that happens."

"Oh, Gio..." she began in exasperation.

"A certain way," he murmured. He took her elbow and pushed her back up the beach, one hand guiding her bottom—as if it couldn't manage on its own, she thought angrily. "Because you're going to help me. And when you've been a good girl and praised me to high heaven," he said, his voice oozing an unnerving triumphant confidence, "then Mother will come to live with me."

"No she won't. She... Gio, you have to realize," Tina said uncomfortably, "she doesn't want to see you."

"She'll change her mind," he said confidently.

Tina groaned. "I'm afraid that's unlikely."

He was ignoring her, relaxing on the ground by her bag, putting his sunglasses to one side, then stripping off his jacket and shirt and laying them carefully on the hot sand to dry. Resenting his takeover bid on her bit of beach, she sat a short distance away and watched the play of his muscles. Then, to her shock, he removed his pants to reveal a pair of cream boxer shorts and a pair of protein-packed thighs.

Tanned, she thought absently. Every bit of him was the most beautiful shade of brown, a cross between caramel and toffee. She felt the warmth of the sun heating her body and relaxing it at the same time, and stretched out her legs to dry them, wishing he didn't look as though he was settled for the day.

"It's wonderful to be back," he said huskily, stretching out on the sand luxuriously. "I've thought of nothing else. Like a bite?" he asked cheerfully, holding out her tuna melt.

Her mutinous eyes lifted. "Oh, yes," she said, eyeing his hand meaningfully.

"The sandwich." He grinned, leaning forward and letting it touch her mouth temptingly, his own lips parting in encouragement.

"*My* sandwich!" she said tartly, snatching it away and taking a huge bite.

"Love a girl with a healthy appetite," drawled Giovanni, and she couldn't answer because her mouth was full.

It was plain from his expression that he was thinking of another kind of healthy appetite. He'd told her once, after she'd flung herself joyfully into his arms, how wonderful it was to be with her, after dating one or two reserved New England society types.

Neither of them had mentioned Beth, who was cool and correct. Tina had always admired Beth's ladylike demeanor and had tried hard to be like her. It had never occurred to her that a man might prefer someone warmer and more outgoing. Giovanni had hinted that Beth had been too prim for his tastes, and his remarks had been a secret delight to Tina. Suddenly she'd been freed from her inhibitions, gaining in confidence and the way she'd felt about herself.

With hindsight and experience, she realized now that Giovanni probably tailored his chat lines to suit whatever woman he was with. Her mouth grew wry. He'd reaped the benefits of telling her how much he liked passionate women. When they were alone she had abandoned the demure protests she'd felt obliged to make for decency's sake and had just enjoyed him—his touch, his skill in arousing her, the intense feelings in her young athletic body.

Munching away now, she ruthlessly crushed the hunger inside her for a man who knew how to make love, who knew how to please her and who found her totally irresistible. Men like that didn't exist, she told herself flatly.

Yet...she ached to be given flattering compliments from Giovanni's silver tongue. She felt the surface of her skin prickle, knowing his fingers were near enough to reach out and touch her. She shifted her body and stared in confusion at the glinting sheet of water protected from the ferocity of the Atlantic by the long spit of land that hooked down like a giant arm from the northern marshes.

Children laughed and squealed at the edge of the freezing sea, teenagers played Frisbee, lovers wandered along the shoreline oblivious to everything around them. A scene of bliss. She should have been bathed in peaceful bliss by now. Instead, she was becoming increasingly edgy. And he'd commandeered her bag with her car keys inside. She should have hung it around her neck!

"Your clothes will be dry soon," she said coldly. "You've had your fun. Now go."

"You think I'm satisfied just with seeing you squirm and wriggle around like a mermaid in heat?" he asked insolently. "I want a lot more than that." His fingers were playing up and down her arm in a maddeningly erotic rhythm that made her want to writhe in delight. And she could feel her breath becoming ragged as a wicked finger drifted up her hip and to the dip at her waist.

"Don't!" she said shortly. "Mermaids aren't for mortals."

Tina made to move away, but he caught her around the waist with both hands. A small shiver went through her body as his breath whispered over the back of her neck. "You'll not turn from me this time," he said with soft mean menace. "If you try, I'll bring the hell back into your life where it rightly belongs."

"I won't help you," she flung at him.

"You will when I've finished with you," he returned softly. His mouth pressed to her spine—warmth on heat, satin on silk. It wandered while he murmured, and his hands held her rigid, and she grew tenser and tenser with the effort of not crying out and releasing the great groan of pleasure that wanted to erupt from her throat. "Yes," he said confidently in her ear. "You will."

Free at last, and wishing she wasn't, she glanced over her shoulder at him and tried to produce a scowl. "What makes you think that?" she asked curtly.

A slow smile lifted the corners of his mouth, and she snapped her head back so that she didn't turn around and fulfill her overwhelming urge to meet his lips with hers in a forever kiss.

"Because I have a fierce hunger that needs satisfying. A motivation to achieve what I want," he said softly. "Look, Tina. Take a look at that mother and child just there."

Puzzled by the connection, Tina swiveled around a little. The woman was smiling gently while the little boy solemnly patted the top of his bucket and lifted it off to display a sand castle. Their shared laughter and pride at the successful result made Tina's heart melt. Even Giovanni's expression was heart-wrenching, as though his love of children had been frustrated, she thought wistfully.

"So?" she asked casually.

"That's what I see everywhere I go. The love of a mother and her son. A sharing of lives. I hold my mother in the highest regard. She and Father sacrificed everything for me, and I gave them everything I possibly could in exchange."

"I know that," she said awkwardly. He might be a rat where women were concerned, but he'd always been willing to shop or do jobs for his parents, even at the expense of his own leisure time. The closeness of his family, the hugs they'd shared, even in public, had been touching to see. There had been no holding back of emotion. Love filled their lives and had been openly expressed. She winced, understanding a little more the trauma that had smashed his life.

"I want her back," he said simply. "I'm prepared to do anything to achieve that." His hand touched Tina's shoulder and she jumped, meeting his eloquent eyes and finding herself mesmerized. The hand began to caress her hot skin. "If you have Sicilian blood you don't do anything by halves."

She shivered, knowing what he was trying to drive into her brain. A sense of respect, born of fear. His fingers were in her hair and she almost—almost—leaned her head back to encourage him. Instead, she shook her head free, sending beads of water flying in all directions. And felt his tongue, touching to each drop he could find on her neck...shoulder...arm....

Tongue-tied herself, she sat mutely, wondering why she wasn't stopping him, and ashamed to admit she knew the answer to that as the arousing sensation of the moist tip of his tongue tormented her with every delicate swoop.

"I think she will find it hard to turn me away when she sees me," he said huskily. "There's a home waiting for her and it's almost ready for her to move in."

Move in. Tina blinked stupidly. He had a house for his mother and he hadn't taken the hint that he was deeply unwelcome. "No," she said unhappily.

"You must understand how much this means to me," he crooned, stroking the back of her neck. And he was closer now, somehow, his honey gold face so near hers that they could be cheek to cheek if she leaned sideways a fraction.... She leaned. It was wonderful, like nuzzling heavy satin. "I've wanted to come back for a long time, Tina," he said quietly, his breath feeding her mouth. "It's possible to forget your home for a while, but then you begin to suffer withdrawal symptoms. I grew up in Palermo and I went there to live when I got out of jail, but Eternity is my home because it's where I began to live. Really live," he continued, his voice filled with intensely felt emotion. "That's why I arranged for an agent of mine to buy a house on my behalf."

Blankly she turned her face and her lips brushed his smooth skin. For a moment, she felt the tug of desire that pulled her to him and the tug of her conscience that drew her away, and she hovered between the two equal forces, her eyes huge and a searing blue, framed by thick black lashes that sparkled with tiny drops of water. And then he was kissing her, sweetly, gently, like the old Gio.

But he wasn't sweet and never had been. She jerked away, the expression in her eyes hurt and betrayed when she remembered what he'd been saying. "A house?" She frowned. "But your mother won't ever live in it with you. She'd never leave Eternity!"

"Ah. So she *is* in Eternity, at least. Well, she wouldn't have to leave," he said, his eyes mocking her unnervingly. "The house is in Eternity."

Tina choked. She felt Giovanni's hand thumping her back and it was some time before she recovered. By then, his hand had begun to stroke her neck again, and he'd moved closer, crooning soothingly as she fought for breath.

"Giovanni, I thought we'd been through all that. You *can't* come back here! You're a—"

"Don't say it!" he warned. The hand lay there, still and heavy. Almost . . . pressing, she thought in alarm. "In your heart, that small forgotten part of you that you keep under lock and key, you know it isn't true," he continued quietly. "I have a whole load of faults, some I'm ashamed of, others that make me who I am. But I've never lied and I've never behaved dishonorably toward a woman in my entire life, no matter how cheaply she holds herself, no matter what the provocation."

"You liar!" she breathed, wishing desperately that he would at least admit what he'd done. "You can't deny—"

"I'll deny it till the day I die," he said softly. "And beyond."

"You were as guilty as hell!" she cried miserably.

He gripped her shoulders and held her at arm's length, fixing her with his fierce black eyes. "That," he said softly, "is not true, and I won't allow you to say it ever again."

The words had been clipped of their usual graceful cadences as they slid through his clenched teeth, and she saw that he was determined to carry out this mad scheme of coming to live in Eternity, whatever pain it caused everyone.

Appalled, Tina gave a low groan of despair. "Where is this house?" she demanded shakily.

"By the wharf, near the town landing. Where Beth and her parents used to live. The Azariah Tamblyn place," he said with a sickeningly smug smile.

CHAPTER FOUR

LAUGHTER BURST from her throat, surprising both of them. "You've blown it!" she cried in triumph. "I suppose you saw it for sale in the realtor's window and thought you'd pick on that house to trick me into cooperating with you. It's true that Beth's parents have sold the Tamblyn place," she said, omitting to mention that they'd lost most of their fortune lately and were moving to somewhere small. *That* would have given Giovanni too much pleasure to hear. "Unfortunately for you, I know who bought it. Patience Powell told me. A car salesman. At just under a million dollars."

"Please! My wallet is still in mourning. You don't get three hundred years of history cheaply," he said ruefully.

"Give me a break," she said derisively. "I've caught you out in a lie, Giovanni. Don't pretend you're in that league."

"Oh," he said, lying back on the sand lazily and resting his head on his raised arms. "I *am* in that league," he murmured drowsily. "Being deprived of everything you've always wanted through no fault of your own—including the woman you love—can really concentrate the mind."

Tina winced. The woman he loved. Something speared through her heart. He'd loved Beth, then, really loved her. Beth had been speaking the truth. She, Tina, had been merely a casual interlude. A bit of fun. She felt quite shocked. It was as if someone had slammed a door in her face. Way in the back of her mind she'd always kidded herself that Giovanni had felt some affection for her, or he couldn't have said all the things he did. His plans for marriage sometime in the future when they'd gotten through school had seemed genuine at the time. He'd *seemed* utterly devoted. But his heart had been given to Beth; and his motives toward *her* had been sexual, nothing more.

Now Tina knew for sure, and it was a salutary lesson. Her anger with him became more focused. Guilt was making him seek out his mother again, not love. He didn't know *how* to love, she thought waspishly. And Adriana, dear sweet Adriana, was better off without him.

"I don't buy your implausible story," she said coldly. "And you haven't bought the Tamblyn place. Patience described the man who did and—"

"Tall, slim, about forty-five, gray haired, very sophisticated, well dressed, talks softly and with an Italian accent. My agent, Antonio Bruscatti," he said sardonically.

Tina's eyes rounded. Bang on! Yet . . . it couldn't be true! A million dollars? "This guy is your agent?" she asked, dumbfounded.

"And a car salesman. He's in charge of my new Boston branch. You'll believe me when I move in."

She eyed him in horror. It would be the kind of ironic twist he'd find amusing. Buying the house where Beth had "queened" it, as he'd so cynically put it once, would give him a good feeling inside. Acquiring it from Beth's parents would be even more of a coup, because he would sweep in there with his elegant suits and slinky Italian car while they suffered the ignominy of taking an apartment by the pizza place. A fitting revenge for people who helped put him in jail. So, she thought with a shiver, what about her punishment? Her eyes silvered with fear.

There was an insufferable smile of contentment on Giovanni's face, which made her believe he was rich. Incredibly rich. Money and power had given him that air of confidence and ease. Grudgingly she admitted to herself that even without taking up his place at Harvard, even with a prison background, he'd be clever enough to claw his way to the top and achieve his ambitions. To be rich, to have power, to *be* somebody. The Lamborghini could easily be his, given his links with the car trade. And the designer suit and the Rolex.

Giovanni had made a fortune. How was another matter.

"Good grief!" she breathed.

A broad grin flashed in her direction. "I'm still a little stunned," he admitted. "I've coveted that house since the day I first saw it, almost fifteen years ago. Like other things I saw and coveted," he continued softly.

"Oh, God!" she moaned in dismay.

It felt as though everything solid in her life was crumbling. Having Giovanni around would be a living hell. Unless she stopped him.

His mouth grew very determined. "You hate the idea, I can see," he said quietly. "But I will not walk away this time. It's part of my plan to pull my life back into shape again. I'm going to live in that house and so is my mother, and everyone will respect me."

"You have dreams that can't come true," she said huskily.

He smiled as if he'd prove her wrong, and to her shame she felt a twinge of envy. "No. I've done with dreaming," he said. "Now I can make them come true. I'm coming back in a big way. Once I was poor. Now I'm wealthy and I can buy my stake in Eternity. I can buy the things my mother loves, and even if she's not sure about her feelings for me, I might be able to coax her to come and talk to me in the garden at Tamblyn. And we'll sit under the cucumber magnolia trees and I'll tell her she can come to live with me. That garden and her love for me will overcome any obstacles."

It seemed so foolproof. The plan had been to give his mother two of her dreams: a wonderful garden and the return of her once-adored son. Under any other circumstances he'd have won his mother over without any trouble at all.

Tina sighed. When she'd gone there for a charity function with his mother once, they'd ignored the speeches and the food and had wandered for hours through all the secret places. A happy time. Like the days when they'd worked contentedly in the little plot at the back of the Kowalski house, united in their love of plants.

"You can't buy her. You can't buy happiness," she said tritely.

"I'm buying time," he drawled. "And perhaps my money can do you a favor. I'm in a buying mood. I see your grandfather's garage is for sale—"

"Forget it! He wouldn't sell it to you if you were the last man on earth!" she said hotly, slanting her gaze at him and wondering how rich he really was. He certainly looked wealthy. Even half-naked he had that kind of "just been groomed by a thousand slaves and never lifted a manicured finger" look. Or could it just be his incredible vanity that kept him busy at the mirror and some male beauty salon in Milan?

Giovanni grinned wryly. "I imagine you'd make damn sure your grandfather was deprived of the chance to sell to me. But it occurred to me," he said with a sly look at her, "that he might be worried if I bought the site next to his."

"He wouldn't like seeing you next door, that's for sure. But why would he be worried?" Tense and anxious, Tina sat more upright. From the tone of his voice, Giovanni was hatching some ghastly plan.

"Because I'd build a classic-car showroom on it," he told her calmly. "I'm a specialist car dealer. Buying, selling, rentals, service and repairs. Sicily, Rome, Milan, New York and lately Boston. I saw that Eternity is knee-deep in the wedding trade and—"

"Yes, Weddings, Inc. has been running successfully for more than a year now," she said.

"Well, it occurred to me that I could rent out classic cars as a sideline. Rolls-Royces. Ferraris. Bentleys. So much more elegant than stretch limos, don't you think?"

She stared at him in astonishment, imagining the students renting his cars, too, for their school proms. And loving the quality cars. "Are you on the level?" she squeaked. He'd apparently bought the Tamblyn place. Why not the

Alden place, too? she thought, and felt her stomach plummet.

His hand pressed against his left breast and he gave her a solemn look. "As level as wine in a glass," he replied.

"If you bought it, the town council would refuse you permission to develop it," she said boldly. "You're not exactly the blue-eyed boy around here."

"They'd be fools not to welcome me as a high-class trader," he replied. "But that's unimportant. The mere fact that one of the biggest garage developers in Europe owned that site would stop any sane person from buying Dan Murphy's garage as a going concern." He smiled at her with false sympathy that made her burn inside. "I'd run an auto-repair business on my site, as well, you see. A gas station, a drive-in and a do-it-all service." He smirked. "There'd be no need for two garages side by side, would there?"

"You bastard!" she said incredulously. "Grandpa's done nothing to hurt you."

"But you have," Giovanni said with soft menace.

Tina went white. "I see."

"You can help me to win my mother over," said Giovanni. "If you don't, your grandfather will be stuck with a business he can't sell. And he'll get older and feebler and the place will slowly fall about your ears with never a buyer in sight."

Astounded at his scheming, she was lost for words. He thought it would be so simple. Throw money at everyone, buy up or destroy the opposition, and life would be dandy.

He was in for a shock. "Your planning's impeccable," she acknowledged coldly. "Unfortunately there's a factor you haven't taken into account."

He sat up, brushing sand from his sleeves. "I've moved a few mountains in my time. Tell me," he said expansively. "Watch me overcome it." He grinned arrogantly at her and suddenly she wanted to wipe that cocky smile away because he believed it was acceptable to ride roughshod over everyone to achieve what he wanted.

A short sharp shock, she thought. It would work—and at least her grandfather and Adriana wouldn't be there to witness it. His plans were so far advanced that he'd have to learn about Adriana, after all. But in knowing about her, he'd abandon his plans to settle because he'd realize his mother would never, ever forgive him. And in that event, Adriana would be perfectly safe. Gio would never want her or the responsibility, and he'd never be able to force the courts to give him custody, not in a million years.

"Come back to my apartment," she said huskily. "I have something to show you."

DRIVING BACK with Giovanni a short distance behind, Tina did her best to concentrate on the road and not the fact that she was about to confront him with the consequences of his past behavior. And she wondered if he'd ever forgive himself—or her, for not contacting him with the news.

She would spell out the truth—that she and Adriana loved one another, that she was more capable of providing the right sort of care and love and he and his money came nowhere in the matter. It would be a terrible blow to him and he'd suffered so much, but she had to stay strong, show him that if he messed with people's lives he'd get hurt in return.

She was alone in this. It was her fight and she was alone.

"For the last time," she said quietly, when they stood outside the apartment again. "I ask you from the bottom of my heart, Gio, and for your own good. Will you leave Eternity now this minute and never return?"

"No. I won't give up my plans. Why do you want me out of your hair so badly, Tina?" he asked softly.

In helpless resignation, she opened the door and walked in, grabbing the railing for support. "Because you won't like what you're going to see," she whispered.

He looked down at her, his expression forbidding. "Show me," he said with a frown. Then he drew a harsh breath. "You're married!" He grabbed her hand roughly, searching it, found it ringless. "A lover?" he barked.

"Come upstairs."

This was it, thought Tina, dry mouthed. The moment of truth. He had a right to know. But... Slowly she ascended with him, wishing a thunderbolt would come. Panic was making her irrational. Perhaps this had been a mistake. Perhaps Adriana would be taken from her. Something close to a sob hovered in Tina's throat. He mustn't even take her on a trip. The poor darling would be bewildered and distraught away from everything familiar and the people she loved.

No. That was stupid. She'd thought that out. No one was in a stronger position than she. Dozens of people would testify to the relationship she had with Adriana. She'd made the right choice, and she was protecting Adriana even now because she would stop Gio from ruining their lives. The lesser of two evils. Her decision was sound.

Yet her misery wouldn't lift, and she stumbled upstairs with Giovanni's fingers closed around her wrist like a vise. Perhaps the only person in trouble was herself. He'd explode. He'd eat her alive, she thought, shivering with nerves.

At the top of the stairs, Giovanni paused and cast a puzzled eye over the bobbing bunch of colorful balloons that had heralded Adriana's birthday a few days ago with so much laughter and merriment. Tina's heart fluttered at the darkness in his eyes, but he only gave the balloons a brief glance and made no comment.

"Dan!" he called loudly.

"I told you. Grandpa's not here," she mumbled.

"Just checking."

Giovanni strode into the small sitting-cum-dining room, hauling her behind him like a naughty child—and stopped dead in his tracks, as she knew he would. Clearly baffled, he took in the label on the door leading to the kitchen. It said KITCHEN in big black felt-pen letters. His head swiveled around, his attention caught by the large black arrow pointing the way they'd come with the words OUT, BEDROOM and BATHROOM on it. There were labels on the drawers for tapes and videos, and brief lists of the contents of the sideboard.

"Teen . . . Your grandfather gone senile?" he asked.

"No." At last the fingers around her hand were loose and inattentive. Even when she slipped free, he didn't seem to notice. She checked the escape route and wondered if she'd need to fling herself down the stairs when . . .

"What the hell is going on?" He frowned, totally perplexed.

She couldn't answer. He shot a look at her white face with its miserable expression and began to prowl around, a half-tamed jungle cat, she thought, watching the liquid movement of his limbs.

"I'll make you a coffee," she said huskily, her pulses racing so fast that she marveled it was possible to move normally.

"Primary readers?" he queried sharply, lifting two cheerfully bright books from the pile of romantic fiction she'd collected in the library sale.

"Yes, Gio," she said nervously. The penny would drop soon. He'd already picked up Adriana's notebook.

"Eat breakfast," he read, managing to decipher the childish writing. "Do teeth. Going out? Are you dressed? Have a look! How's your hair? Brush—" He broke off. "What the hell is this, Tina?" he demanded, but she only stared helplessly at him, her big black-fringed eyes glistening with tears. He bent his head to the notebook again and read the rest. "—is on your dressing table in the bedroom. Do you need a coat, outdoor shoes, a purse? Is it raining? Take an umbrella or swim!" He scowled at Tina. "Whose is this? What the hell is going on?"

"Coffee!" she yelped, and fled.

He followed close on her heels in a hot scrambling rush, and she felt the panic rising within her. But he stopped short and stretched out a hand to examine the label tied to the handle of the kettle on the countertop. He muttered something under his breath, apparently no closer to solving the mystery.

"I suppose you remembered to put water in?" he read. "Put me on the gas and I'll be in trouble!" Tina spilled coffee all over the counter. He'd now begun to examine Adriana's second notebook, the one that she kept by the bed and brought in to breakfast every morning. "Get up. Wash. Dry yourself or feel soggy! Do teeth. Dress for the day (is it warm? cold?). Take medication. Go into kitchen and pick up red notebook for more." He let out a small grunt. "It goes on and on! You got someone's kid staying here? They're very organized," he said suspiciously.

"No, Gio. Not someone's kid." Carefully, holding her own hand to stop it shaking, she spooned the coffee into the mugs. "Damn! I've forgotten to switch on the kettle!" she muttered.

Giovanni began to read out the notice that hung from the central light fixture. "Is the gas on? Are you cooking? Look around, check that everything is safe . . ." He took her arms firmly and turned her around, an expression of sheer bewilderment on his face. "Tina—"

"Wait for the coffee and I'll explain," she said unhappily. She could see his quick mind turning things over. He'd get it in a moment.

"You didn't want me to stay around. You were reluctant to bring me up here," he said slowly. "You were scared of what I'd see. A kid's reading book. A routine for getting up. Labels for an idiot . . ." Tina winced. He was working it out logically, step by step. "Or a kid. You're looking after . . ."

He stiffened and his grip became like bonded steel. Behind them the kettle whistled loudly, but she couldn't move a muscle to turn it off because she was mesmerized by the sudden leap of understanding in his eyes.

"Gio," she mouthed, her voice momentarily locked into a terrible silence. "Gio?" she whispered uncertainly, feeling him relax and seeing the great inhalation of breath expanding his chest.

"Oh, Tina!" he growled, his voice shaking with emotion. "You fool! You should have searched for me, found me, told me! My mother has my address." She looked at him stupidly as he shook his head in apparent exasperation. "You ought to have told me. I had a right to know," he said gently. "I know what you were so scared of, but you had nothing to fear. This is my responsibility, as well as yours."

"Oh." That was it. For a moment she felt blank and numb, almost as though this was an anticlimax. All this time she'd feared his reaction, but it had been easier than she'd thought! No drama, no blind anger. She let out a long groan of utter relief. "Thank God you've taken it like this!" she cried jerkily.

To her total astonishment, he crushed her in a bear hug and then tilted her chin up to kiss her, slowly, beautifully, a wealth of affection and meaning in the endless embrace. And, as he always had done in moments of intense passion, he began to murmur to her in slow languorous Italian, words that accompanied his tender kisses and the gentle movement of his hands on her back. The kiss of a lover, she thought distractedly. Too sweet to be bearable.

Was he kissing her and taking it so well because he felt overwhelmed and grateful? she wondered in confusion. Did he realize what a sacrifice she must have made? A rush of compassion rolled through her body. All this time he'd never known. It must be a terrible shock and her heart went out to him.

"Gio..." she began nervously, discovering that he was kissing her with a rising intensity and that his hands were moving lower and lower, now rotating over her small rear. She cringed against him and that was a mistake, her face aflame with scarlet when she felt the hard male pressure against her body. So she tried wriggling sideways and he interpreted that as a sensual writhe, groaning in his throat. "Stop! Stop this now!" she pleaded.

"No, don't. Please don't stop me from holding you, Tina," he muttered between the raining kisses. "I need this. Oh, God, how I need this!"

"I know you're upset," she whispered against his satin cheek, as his mouth roamed the acutely sensitive skin of her throat. He muttered thickly, pushing her against the stove, bending her backwards. "But you can't do this. Please! I . . . I'm sorry for what you're going through, but . . . Oh, Gio!" she gasped.

The intimacy of his tongue stopped her words, the heat of his body moulded to hers. Fiercely he kissed her, unstoppable now, his groan of need unlocking her and opening her up willingly, wantonly, to his impassioned caresses. Her hand lifted to grasp his hair and the soft silky curls clung to her fingers as though they wanted to secure her tightly.

"You feel gorgeous," he whispered roughly, pulling her harder into him, sipping her, savoring the taste of her lips, the sharp edge of her white teeth. And she moaned in her throat, whimpering with pleasure, her whole body flowing into his like the river to the sea, as if it were the most natural thing in the world.

She was doing this, she told her cautioning brain, because he was so torn emotionally. He needed comfort, and she in her warmhearted way was letting him cling to her.

And she was a liar, she thought in despair. She wanted him. He was nothing but a cheat and a two-timer. Her heart missed a beat. She'd have to stop this right now. And what would he do then?

Panic paralyzed her. He wouldn't want to stop now. He'd want more than she was prepared to give. "Stop!" she whispered fiercely. "Before it's too late."

Slowly he drew back, but his eyes weren't angry or simmering with desire. They were gentle, understanding. Tina let out a shudder of relief.

"It's not too late, Tina," he rasped.

"Giovanni," she said. "I'm not sure you—"

"Don't be afraid," he crooned, stroking her face. "I won't push you further than you want to go. Not now." He grinned crookedly. "Not yet. God, I can hardly believe it!"

"No, well, it's true," she admitted.

"I have to apologize . . ."

"Apologize?" she repeated, the joy of hope leaping into her troubled eyes. "Gio, that would make so much difference!"

He ruffled her hair affectionately. "I understand that," he said ruefully. "It must have been hard for you."

She nodded. "Hard, but rewarding."

"No," he murmured, kissing the wet hollows of her eyes, and she closed them in ecstasy, hardly daring to believe that Giovanni would at last find peace of mind. Her decision had brought a startling result. He was mellowing before her very eyes, and she felt certain she could trust him to be tender and loving to Adriana.

Soon, very soon, she thought exultantly, he and Adriana could meet and begin to make a relationship together. It had always been her dearest wish. Then, maybe... She blushed, not daring to hope what might lie in the far-distant future when everyone's hearts had been softened with time....

"Sweet Tina," he said huskily, breaking into her dreams. "I let you down. I thought I'd taken care of things, that... well," he said with a helpless shrug. "I suppose nothing's a hundred percent safe."

"Safe? What do you mean?" she asked slowly, completely baffled.

Giovanni kissed the tip of her nose. "Idiot! You know what I mean. I didn't protect you well enough. The last thing I wanted was to cause you trouble," he said gently, and he shook his head in exasperation at her look of utter bewilderment. "No more teasing," he said. "Tell me. For the love of God, tell me! I can hardly wait to know. Boy or girl?"

"What?" She stared dumbfounded while he continued to smile at her, a quizzical expression on his face. "Boy... or girl?" she repeated stupidly, and he nodded, a depth of tenderness in his eyes that turned her to jelly in his arms.

He smiled in gentle amusement. "You're as dazed as I am! I'm talking about our child. What sex? Boy or girl?" He grinned a little sheepishly. "I don't mind either way. But put me out of my suspense, for pity's sake. Do I have a son or a daughter?''

Tina's puzzled smile was wiped from her face. Sense at last. She let out a strangled cry of horror, her eyes enormous with dismay. "No!" she gasped. "You...you believe that the...labels and the simple reading books are for a child?"

"I always did get straight *A*'s! I wasn't in the gifted class for nothing!" He grinned.

Numb with pain, she shut her eyes to shield herself from the look on his face. A child—*their* child! And like any Italian, for whom children are life and breath and the whole purpose of living, he was overjoyed to think he'd become a father and would forgive her anything because she'd supposedly borne his child.

He hadn't understood at all. He'd kissed her and held her only because he thought there was someone at last who could love him unquestionably and not remember his crime, his shame. Tina's groan came from deep inside her. That was why he'd been overcome with emotion. Someone of his own to love. All his tender words, the sweet talk, had only surfaced because he wanted to take a lion's share of his child and he knew that her cooperation was essential to his purpose.

"Oh, Gio!" she said hopelessly.

"Oh." He grinned, and with that dazzling, melting smile came another flow of Italian that sounded like caresses and ate into her vulnerable heart.

"Please..." Thick choking emotions filled her throat again. She would have loved to have his baby, she realized, in one dreadful flash of knowledge. The ache began for what she could never achieve and her lip started to quiver.

"What is it, Tina?" he asked gently.

"There...is no...child," she said in a pathetic little voice.

A small frown drew his brows together. "Oh, come on, Tina! You can't hide the facts," he said with an edge of irritation.

"There is no child," she repeated miserably. "I don't have a child. I never did." *And I never will,* she thought with a self-pitying sniff.

His jaw tightened. "I see," he grated through his teeth. "That's how it's to be, is it? I'm not stupid! I can see the evidence! We'll prove that a child lives here." Roughly he bundled her unresisting body out of the room, pushing her toward one of the doors on the landing. "It's locked," he said curtly, after trying the handle. "Key."

"You've got them," she muttered, wincing under the pressure of his fingers.

Eventually thrusting the right key into the lock, he pushed the door hard, and it shuddered open under the onslaught of his fist. It was obviously her grandfather's room, and the next one he tried, the little room, was obviously hers.

"Why bother to lock internal doors?" he demanded suspiciously, turning from her neatly made bed, the pretty dressing table and the cherished pictures of her parents in their school in Puerto Rico.

"Security," she mumbled.

"Huh!" Giovanni glared and strode grimly to the last door.

"Calm down!" she cried anxiously. "For God's sake, calm down, Giovanni!"

"I want to see the evidence. And you might tell me where my child is!" he growled, fiddling ineffectually with the key.

Tina knew the door was unlocked—a fact he hadn't even checked—but she said nothing, needing time to placate him. "The labels and books and messages weren't for a child," she insisted in as composed a manner as possible. But she wanted to weep. Fear for herself, fear for Adriana. And, to her surprise, sorrow for him and what he'd lost by one mindless action.

"Where is my child?" he demanded tightly.

"There is no child!" she wailed, her heart half breaking.

"Damn you!" he cried, abandoning the fruitless struggle with the key and shaking her. "Open this! I want to see for myself! And then you can tell me where he—she—is!"

"No, I—"

"You bitch!" he raged. "Tell me! Tell me, Tina! I won't let you keep my flesh and blood from me!"

"I have no child!" she yelled in despair.

"Tell me!" he roared.

"No child!" she sobbed. "Please, stop it, Gio! You're breaking my heart."

"Tell me! Tell me!" he demanded relentlessly. "I'll shake you till your body falls apart! For the love of God, where is my child?"

"Leave me alone!" she said jerkily. "I can't think! You're hurting me!"

"I don't want to hurt you," he said tightly. "But you can't torture me like this. I have a right to know about my own child, don't I?"

"Oh, God, Gio, there is no child! *No* child! Can't you see? Haven't you grasped it yet?"

"Grasped what?" he snapped contemptuously. "That you've kept my child—"

"For the last time," she cried hysterically, "there is no child! It's...it's...your *mother!*" she answered hysterically.

He let her go so suddenly that she had to grab frantically at the banister, her head spinning dizzily. And she half sank to the floor, her legs reduced to a mass of unsupported flesh.

"My *mother?*" he cried hoarsely. "*Madonna,* what are you saying?"

Slowly she hauled herself up, hand over hand, her fingers gripping the hard wooden struts till she could stand upright and meet his horrified eyes. "It's not locked. The door's open," she said weakly.

Grimly he turned on his heel and went inside Adriana's room, looking around expectantly as if he was sure he'd see his child there. Or toys, a baseball bat, posters of pop stars, a pair of roller skates. Anything to prove her wrong.

The room held none of those, of course. And then he sniffed, picking up the scent of lavender that Tina had always associated with his mother ever since Adriana and

Lech Kowalski had arrived from Sicily with the devastatingly attractive Giovanni and turned her world upside down. She let out a small sob. Now he knew.

Exhausted and spent, Tina leaned her listless body against the banister. "Now will you believe me?" she asked dully.

"This is the window with bars on," he said, a tight line to his mouth, a fury in the black eyes.

"That's right."

She waited, drained, hurting, aching inside. Slowly he checked the room through and obviously he recognized one or two things because he picked up objects now and then, a cold expression on his strained face.

"*Madonna, madonna . . . Impossible . . .*"

It was only too possible, and it made her feel inexpressibly sad to watch him fingering some of the frocks in the tiny wardrobe. Her hand moved to press hard against the tightness in her lungs when he leaned forward and buried his nose in the pretty dresses that smelled so sweetly of lavender.

"I'm sorry, Gio," she said feebly, wishing convention allowed her to take him in her arms and rock him soothingly.

His shoulders lifted in tension. His movements became slower and slower till he'd come to a total halt and was standing in the middle of the room like a mindless zombie.

"I thought . . ." he began, but his husky voice cracked and Tina's compassionate heart went out to him. He'd hoped for a child. Instead, he'd discovered that something quite incomprehensible had happened to his mother. "I thought we . . ." He gulped and it was a moment before he could go on. "Dear God!" he muttered almost inaudibly. "No . . . child at all?"

Too upset to speak, she shook her head. Her eyes strayed to the picture on the landing table of her sister, Sue, and baby Michael, the child Gio had killed, and a raw sob tore from her throat. "No child at all!" she whispered, and there was an emptiness in his face, a rawness about his eyes, that came close to breaking her into a thousand pieces.

CHAPTER FIVE

GIOVANNI VISIBLY struggled to pull himself together, although high spots of color burned on his cheeks as he followed her gaze to the photograph. A huge breath lifted his rib cage. "*Non capisco*. I don't understand."

"Go into the sitting room," she said huskily. "I'll bring the coffee."

Her hand was trembling badly, so she put the cups on a small carved tray that had once belonged to Adriana's Polish husband. When she reached the sitting room door, her eyes filled with tears. Giovanni was sitting in an armchair staring into space, and his handsome face was as still and as cold as deeply etched stone. It was obvious that he was making a huge effort to hold back his emotions, his big hands clenching as though he wanted to hit someone and release some of his frustration with life.

"I would have liked a child." The words were stark and hard, a statement of fact without the color of emotion at all. His control was astounding—and rather frightening. But he was hurting inside, she knew. He'd made a fool of himself and he'd be seething with self-anger for that alone.

"I know," she mumbled, turning from her image of their shared child. It was too seductive, too lovely to contemplate—and too cruelly ironic that the man who'd killed her niece should wish his child on her.

"Where is my mother?" he asked without looking up.

"Touring, with Grandpa." She stood awkwardly, shifting from one foot to the other. What did you say at a time like this? Normally she had a word of comfort for all occasions. Whatever troubles her students had brought to her, they'd always gone away feeling easier and more able to cope. This time she felt tongue-tied. It was awful to learn that your mother was no longer the person you'd known. He was waiting for her to expand. Bravely she tried. "Adriana—your mother—is fine," she said gently to reassure him. "Very fit and cheerful."

"Why do you keep her a prisoner?" he snarled.

"We don't—"

"There are bars on the window!" he snapped. "My mother's just seventy and I doubt she's into sneaking off at night." He scowled. "Unless she's a reluctant guest here! Does she try to get out?"

Tina stared at him numbly. Often enough, she thought. Didn't he understand? It seemed so obvious to her, but then she knew. She must tell him slowly, gently.

"What the hell are you doing with her? Why is she here at all?"

"She came a couple of years ago. She needs company," she said quietly. "You know that she and Grandpa always were good friends." Giovanni's liquid black eyes met hers and she shivered to see how bleak they looked. "Here." She poured some brandy into their cups. "You've had a shock." Tina gratefully sipped the coffee and waited for the brandy to warm her through and give her courage to continue. "The bars are for her safety. She's prone to falling. You know how elderly ladies are." Giovanni smoothed his hand over his hair, brooding on that. "And she sleepwalks."

He met her eyes sharply. "She never did before."

"It's . . . it's a reaction to shock," said Tina delicately.

There was a flash of fury in the glittering eyes and then, "Those memo-aids. They're hers?" he asked curtly.

Tina nodded and took another reviving sip of the smooth Italian coffee, trembling because he was watching her warily, his dark eyes fixed on her. "You . . . had no idea she'd come to live here, then?" she asked cautiously, trying to swing the conversation in another direction. "Her family in Palermo . . ."

"That's one of the reasons I'm here," he explained, with a frown that drew his dark brows together at fierce angles. Tina saw from his dazed eyes that he still hadn't quite gotten over the shock of imagining he had fathered a child and discovering that it was his mother whom Tina was caring for. No wonder his quick mind wasn't working to its usual capacity. "When relatives phoned her house, a stranger answered. And she denied all knowledge of my mother."

"That would be Jim Falconer's grandmother," she said quietly. "She doesn't know your mother's forwarding address."

"Falconer?" He frowned again.

"Distant relative of Katherine's."

He grunted. "We assumed Mother was ashamed of what had happened and that's why she stopped answering our letters."

"They're here," she said quietly. "The mailman redirects her stuff." She pulled the stool to the high cupboard and stood on it, reaching up to the box she'd hidden away. "Yours are here, too. I hid them because Adriana would have destroyed them, and I thought that would be a pity," she explained, seeing the query in his eyes as she handed them down to him. "One day..." Her voice shook and she forced herself to stay in control of her emotions. "One day I thought she might be willing to read them."

Stony faced, he riffled through the letters, discovering the ones he'd written in the beautiful copperplate handwriting she'd always admired, wishing she had his artistic streak. There was a huge stack of them, all unopened.

"I wrote every week," he growled. "I didn't really expect to have a reply, but I did imagine she'd been reading my news. For God's sake, Tina, what have you done to make her hate me for so long? Have you been keeping those deaths constantly at the forefront of her mind?" he demanded angrily, surrounded by the sad heaps of his unwanted letters.

"Me? No, I swear—"

"I can't believe that!" he snarled. "I was the child of her middle years! Her only, long-awaited child. She loved me as only an Italian woman can love her child, and I served my sentence, unjust though it was. I thought," he grated, "she would have forgiven me by now."

Tina wondered if a mother could ever forgive her trusted and beloved son for killing a woman and child and refusing to accept responsibility for his actions. After all, Giovanni had destroyed every one of Adriana's hopes for him—and shattered her blind belief that he was the most wonderful son in the world. He'd broken the Sicilian code of honor, and that had been unforgivable. No wonder Adriana's fragile mind had become troubled beyond its capacity.

It was so sad. So unnecessary. "I tried to interest her in the letters—Grandpa did, too—but she cried and kept pushing them away." Tina took a deep breath, finding it almost impossible to say what she had to. But there was no other way. "Gio, this is difficult to explain, but...I'm afraid your mother loathes the very thought of you. She...she never forgave you for what you did—" She broke off, gasping at the force being exerted on her wrist.

Mutely she pleaded with him for compassion. He gave her none, remorselessly maintaining the pressure. "I did nothing to be ashamed of!" he said tightly. "She'll know that when we've had a talk." Tina felt the tension screwing up every one of her tired muscles. "I'll prove my innocence," he growled.

"But you're not innocent!" she protested.

"I am!" he insisted. "I mean to claw back the life I've lost and regain the affection of my mother. My father's dead and it's too late for him to know I was wrongly accused. But I won't let my mother die unhappy!"

"She's not—"

"She has no son! Have you any idea what that means to a woman of her nationality? She has no son because she disowned him of her own accord. I don't know what that's done to her, but whatever she may show to the world, it won't have made her happy inside!" He turned two black and diamond-hard eyes on her. "And all because two little bitches decided to teach a lesson to a guy they thought had two-timed them."

"No!" she cried, the word wrenched out of her in an agonized protest.

"Still denying the truth? You feel no regrets? No sympathy for what happened to me?" he asked, his eyes brooding on the passion flooding across her upturned face.

"I believe in justice," she replied in a low voice.

"So do I," he agreed with a worrying intensity of feeling. He contemplated her thoughtfully again, his eyes slowly taking in every detail of her small trembling body.

"She won't forgive you!" Tina blurted out with a conviction born of desperation. And contrarily she felt an overwhelming wash of pity. His face had paled noticeably, and the lines around his mouth had deepened with pain. Oh, God! she thought. She *had* to go on, to be cruel, for Adriana's sake. "Get used to that fact," she cried, anxiety making her voice harsh. "If ever she hears your name, she begins to cry and she doesn't stop for hours. You don't know what it's like, Giovanni!"

"You evil little witch!" he growled savagely.

"No, it's all true!" she protested, hating what she was having to say, knowing she must because of the fiercely determined set of his mouth. Adriana's welfare came first. Everyone else's second. "You've never heard her crying, pouring out her hatred of you, how base and sinful and lacking in honor you are!" She was half-hysterical herself. "After she's vented the anger she's bottled up inside, she's exhausted and ill—and so are we. It's unbearable!"

"You don't have to go on. I get the picture," he said in steel-cut tones.

"Please, *please* don't persist with this crazy idea of trying to heal the past," she begged plaintively. "You can't blame me for seeing her side of it more clearly than yours. And she was innocent...."

"Yes," he said, his eyes blazing. "She was innocent and she suffered and for that reason..."

For a heart-stopping moment she thought she'd caught a promise of vengeance in those fierce eyes, but he dropped his lashes before she could be sure. And she decided that he couldn't hold her responsible for his mother's distress. Whatever he said in bravado, he was intelligent enough to know—if not to admit—that it was his own actions that had robbed him of everything he cherished.

He must be hurting so badly, she thought, blinking back the hot pricking tears, ruthlessly swallowing away the hard lump that had risen to block her throat. Giovanni must not confront his mother, and it was up to her to deter him.

"I appreciate the fact that you were hoping your mother was less angry with you and that you'd set your heart on a reunion," she said tremulously. "I can understand how disappointed you are, but you have to back away. If you like," she added in desperation, "I'll write to you and let you know how she is once in a while."

"I don't trust you or your motivations," he muttered grimly. "Mother's house has obviously been sold. It wasn't much, I know—it was on the wrong side of the tracks—but Father worked hard to make it into a palace for Mother and me. Now what I want to know is, how the hell did you persuade her to leave—when she loved her garden so much—and come here, where there's nothing, not even a window box?" He leaned forward, his face dark and intense. "How much control do you have over her affairs, Tina?"

Her heart sank. "Through the lawyer—and with your mother's approval—Grandpa and I have been granted total control," she replied reluctantly.

"Now we're getting somewhere!" he said contemptuously. "You greedy little bitch! You take advantage of an old lonely woman and pocket the little money she has and force her to live in these squalid conditions."

"They're not squalid!" she protested indignantly. "The apartment's clean! And the money's in an account to pay for medical bills."

He left his chair and grabbed her roughly, pulling her to her feet. *"Gesù!"* he growled. "What's wrong?"

Tina was petrified. But she had to tell him. "We all need money for medical bills. Gio," she began gently. "Don't you realize what your behavior did to your mother?"

"Oh, yes," he said bitterly. "Father told me in graphic detail."

He paused, his eyes glittering like black jewels. He was hurting. His pride, his arrogance, had taken a knock. That was obvious from the tight-set line of his jaw, the thinning of his mouth and the rocklike tension in every one of his straining muscles. It was hurting her, too; everything she'd wanted to forget had been thrust back into the forefront of her mind, and she was being brutally forced to relive it all.

"I thought he'd refused to see you," she said, remembering Lech Kowalski's white, white face, the hollow shadows beneath those Slavic cheekbones, the tense pain in his proud mouth. And the anger. The terrible anger.

"He sent a message to my lawyer," said Giovanni shortly. "He told me never to come home again, that I was no longer his son." He eased the crease over his knee, lining it up neatly, as if it was the most important thing on his mind. Tina felt choked. She knew how much he'd loved his father. "And I'll never come to terms with the fact that my father died thinking the worst of me," he finished quietly.

"He was a good man. A proud man, highly respected," she said huskily.

"And I wasn't."

"Not after... not after that day, no," she said shakily.

Her mind strayed to Lech Kowalski, and the delight that had lit his dark face whenever Giovanni was around. How the two, father and son, would go for long walks together or take a punt along the Sussex River to the marshlands, where they'd sit and talk for hours.

Giovanni's fist slammed onto the table, making the cups jump and rattle. "God, Tina! Too many innocent people have suffered in this!"

"I'm glad you realize that," she replied. Her face felt stiff, the tears springing to her eyes. His violent, selfish needs had touched too many lives, ruined too many people.

"I'm laying a lot of things at your door," he ground out.

"What? You're blaming me?"

"When you refused to believe me, all the uncertainty that existed about my guilt was wiped clean away," he growled. "Several people thought they'd heard a car door slam, as if I'd gotten out as I claimed, leaving Beth to drive. Your testimony that you saw me—"

"I did!" she said miserably, wishing she hadn't, wishing she'd been somewhere else, anywhere, but hearing that sickening crunch of metal, watching that terrible scene.

"You saw something and interpreted it incorrectly," he said tightly. "You, and only you, could have stopped that tide of hatred and hysteria—if you'd stopped to listen to me, if you'd come to talk to me when I was out on bail. You, with your wise honesty and sense of fairness. But when you sided with Beth, everyone fell on the dung heap with you. They decided they must have been mistaken about the car door. It would have taken only one person, Tina, and you should have been that person. I am innocent as the day is long and, by God, I'm going to prove it! Yes, I'm blaming you!" His voice had become a yell.

An intense and uncontrollable anger exploded within her, forged in the fire of her Irish heritage and the hot blood of the Spanish tin miners from Ireland's feudal past.

"*Nothing* is your fault, is it?" she yelled back. "Beth shouldn't have been so frigid, I shouldn't have been so available, Beth shouldn't have refused your demands for money, and I should never have seen what I did!"

"That's about it!" he snarled. "Without any of that happening, I wouldn't have lost a mother, a father, a home, a scholarship to Harvard and a promising future."

"Oh." Miserably she thought of his enforced exile and its consequences. And understood why he was so bitter. He'd lost everything that he and his family had held dear; the proud Kowalskis' struggle to sacrifice everything for their clever son had come to nothing, and instead of lifting them all from poverty, he'd driven them deeper into debt and misery.

"Yeah. Oh," he mocked. But there was a terrible pain in the lines that drew down the corners of his mouth and a bleakness in his contemptuous eyes.

Tina swallowed away the huge lump in her throat. "I know it must have been hard."

"Hard?" The eyes leapt to life with a blaze of unquenchable fire. "I had one thing to keep me burning with life. The thought of revenge."

She took a deep breath. "Revenge?" she repeated in horror, her mouth dry. "Not Beth!" she breathed.

"Could be."

"You can't hurt her! You mustn't even see her! It took ages before she pulled herself together," Tina protested. "She fell to pieces after you left."

"She fell on her feet," he corrected laconically. "A nice little arrangement with a society friend in a swish art gallery in Back Bay in Boston and a comfortable apartment by the Charles River."

"How . . . how do you know?"

"I got a trace on her. She's in a bad way. Drinks too much."

"I didn't know. I lost contact. Beth wouldn't speak to me after the trial." Beth and Gio had been close. Tina wondered how he felt, knowing that the woman he loved was an alcoholic. The answer would never be found in the blankness of his expression and in the flat, even tones of his voice. "What are you going to do to Beth?" she demanded.

"For the moment, nothing. I think she's in a private hell of her own, so I'll let her stay there for a while."

"You callous brute!"

"She deserves to be horsewhipped, but I'm concentrating on something more important for the moment," he said. "I've come here to be reunited with my mother. When will she be back?"

Tina groaned in exasperation. He wouldn't listen and she'd have to be cruel, really cruel if she was to keep him away. She took a deep breath and plunged in. "If you turn up out of the blue, you risk killing her with the shock," she said bluntly, and met his gaze head on. This was her last chance before she was forced to tell him the truth.

She summoned all her courage and went on. "Your mother hates you so much that she's destroyed every reminder, every memento of you. Everything. Even her photographs of you as a baby. She wishes you never existed, that she never bore you—"

"Gesù!" he muttered rawly.

"I'm sorry," she whispered, barely holding on to her self-control. "But I had to say it. I care for her and can't allow you to tear her apart with your ideas of a cozy reunion. It just won't work! You ruined her life and she'll never forgive you, never in a million years."

"Tina . . ." he said in a choking voice, and she began to weep silently. "I still have to try. . . ."

Her stomach was clutched with nausea. She held it with unsteady hands, pressing it in, keeping back the desire to run and be sick. "In that case . . . there's something else." She lifted her tearstained face to his. "I'd have given anything, *anything* not to tell you," she whispered, pale and wretched. Her eyes filled again and she furiously rubbed away the bleariness with her knuckles.

"There can't be more," he muttered.

"I'm afraid there is," she replied gently, feeling for him. "Your mother is physically fit, but she's . . . she's suffering from retrograde amnesia."

His eyes narrowed. "What do you mean?" he asked with sinister quietness.

"It's why we need the money. For Lal, the nurse," Tina croaked, upset for herself, upset for him and the loss of all his dreams. "Your mother has forgotten a huge chunk of the past. She knows that you did something terrible and that you trigger off a hysterical reaction in her she can't control. *That's* why you can't live in the same town, because if you're anywhere around she'd have to remain a prisoner in this flat. Not only that," Tina went on jerkily, unable to meet his appalled eyes any longer, "she's a twenty-four-hour responsibility. She doesn't remember if she's eaten, whether she's supposed to be dressing or undressing or where her own room is. She's a helpless woman who needs watching, Giovanni, and her mind is so fragile that she must have fixed routines and people around her who understand and love her and who'll forgive her for repeating the same question, the same phrase or story, over and over again in the course of an evening. She needs patience. She needs love and attention. But she doesn't need you."

He looked blankly at Tina for a few seconds while the silence between them thickened and the tension became almost visible. And then, "My God!" he exclaimed hoarsely. "You stick the knife in, you twist it and calmly slide it out without even checking for blood!"

"You had to be told," she said. "You *made* me tell you!" she yelled resentfully, facing him. "I've been trying to keep you from knowing how bad she's been because, yes, it would be twisting the knife, and I thought you'd probably suffered enough. But you were determined to blunder on, disregarding anyone else but yourself. You can't do that, Giovanni! Your mother's needs come first as far as I'm concerned."

She paused and saw with heart-wrenching anguish how much this was hurting him. Almost as much as it was hurting her. "Oh, this is a living nightmare!" she said tremulously.

"Try mine," he retorted in a tight hard voice.

She swallowed, unwilling to be swayed by his distress, reminding herself it was his punishment. "Be grateful that Adriana's happy enough," she ventured, wanting to make it easier for him to walk away from everything he'd dreamed of. "Grandpa is very fond of her, too, and they play word games together and watch TV. She helps me make cookies and do the vegetables, and she teaches me Sicilian dishes, which she remembers. The specialist said that the mind's like that—holding some memories, abandoning others."

"And what did he say caused this amnesia?" Giovanni asked softly.

She hesitated and then, "You."

He was very still for a long time, and she stayed quiet so that the implications of what she'd told him could sink in. "That's one hell of a workload you've taken on," he muttered at last. His hand briefly stretched out, stroked the side of her face and fell away before she had time to stop the quiver that ran through her. "You could have let her go into a home."

Tina looked at him helplessly. "Never," she said fervently. She'd felt partly responsible. "I'm fond of her. We have fun."

"No wonder you're not the sunny happy woman I once knew."

Tina felt her mouth trembling and going out of shape, so she pulled it back together, but still it drooped. She wanted to say they would both have been happy if he'd stayed with her, instead of two-timing her; if he'd never betrayed the great love she'd saved for him. Instead, she came up with a platitude.

"We're all getting older. With responsibilities."

"What's the prognosis on my mother?" he asked quietly. "Will she recover her memory?"

"There's always hope, the specialist said," she answered wearily. "Frankly, their guess is as good as mine, though she's made quite a lot of progress. I do know that she mustn't be put under stress. Gio, don't you see, if you really love your mother, you have to do the hardest thing and walk away," she said in a plaintive voice. "She *has* improved over the years, and some of her memory is coming back. But she mustn't be driven over the edge by your sudden appearance, not when it was you who..." She gulped at the light that flicked across his eyes. "Not when..."

"Not when I caused her mind to crack," he said softly. "I'm the last person on earth she'd want to live with, aren't I?"

"Oh, Gio!" Tina said brokenly, feeling a little piece of her was dying every second she looked at his haunted face. "Accept that this was a mistake. Turn your back on Eternity and get on with whatever life you've made in Sicily." The tears totally blurred her vision. "Go," she said raggedly, her heart wrenching in anguish. "For God's sake, go!"

He rose as if obeying her like some automaton. "I had no idea," he said huskily. "I'd expected a little opposition, some tears...and then..." He gave a short mirthless laugh. "I thought that tonight I'd be taking Mother out to dinner to celebrate."

"You see how it is, don't you?" she asked anxiously.

Giovanni fixed her with an intense stare. "With great clarity." His eyes bored into hers for a few more seconds and then he looked away. "I will change my plans," he said softly. "Don't bother to get up. I can let myself out. Remember me to your grandfather."

There had been only the faintest crack in his voice, and she marveled at how well he could mask his feelings. The relief swept through her like a great tide and then came a feeling of emptiness. Miserably she knew that her life would never be complete without him and that she ached physically for a man who was worthless.

"You...you can share my lunch if you like," she offered generously, released from anxiety now that he'd decided to leave.

He smiled faintly. "Thank you, no. For me, lunch is from one o'clock to four, not at noon, and it consists of proper food, not a snatched sandwich. Lunch should be...a time for sitting with your family," he said.

In his stone-hard eyes she recognized the signs of the shutters coming down to shield his emotions from others—and to protect himself from their sympathy or scorn. Tina's wretchedness was plain for anyone to see.

His family had always eaten a proper lunch, talking animatedly, compassionately, thoughtfully, a dozen emotions flying over their faces as they ate and laughed and loved together. It was a wonderful ritual, one she dreamed of doing with her own family when she married, because meals at home had always been snatched on the run or taken in slumped exhaustion in front of the television.

Family... she thought wistfully.

"Yes. Family."

Tina started, then looked at him guiltily. "I didn't realize I'd spoken aloud," she said. "I'm sorry. I'd been thinking—"

"So had I." The strain had drawn down the lines of his face. "You never get those golden moments back." Giovanni's eyes narrowed to black stone slits. "Thank you for looking after my mother," he said with stiff politeness. "Goodbye, Tina. Ciao."

Because he looked so cold and remote, because he had given a brief nod of his head, instead of extending his hand, she stayed sitting. His manner didn't invite warmth or the expression of sympathy. He'd retreated into his shell, the aloof suspicious shell he'd worn when he'd first come to Eternity. But her heart ached for him because he was so utterly alone and without the comfort of family love.

"Goodbye," she said shakily, her eyes huge with compassion. "Are you... are you going back to Sicily?"

"No," he said shortly. He paused, contemplating her thoughtfully. "California."

With a puzzled frown, she watched him walk out. California. Her hand froze in the act of reaching for a strawberry. Oh, God! she thought in shock. It might be a coincidence but... that was where the owners of the derelict Alden place lived.

Cold, shaking, Tina stumbled to the window, watching him open the door of the exotic car and climb in without a backward glance, firmly wedging the heavy-framed sunglasses on his aristocratic nose. And though he appeared to be the epitome of a sophisticated and elegant gentleman without a care in the world, she knew from subtle details about his body—the set of his back, the deliberate movements of his tense hands—that he was holding back a terrible rage that would need an outlet before long.

The engine roared angrily into life. He jammed his foot on the accelerator and screamed off the site in a cloud of dust and burning rubber. Yes, he was upset about his mother—and furious that he'd been denied access, she thought nervously as he slewed onto the street.

He only cared about satisfying his own selfish needs. He'd suggested that he'd not only buy the Tamblyn house, but the old Alden place, as well. That would end any hope they had of selling the garage.

That would be his revenge. It was in his grasp and he wasn't the kind of man to let it slip. Okay, so California was a huge state. He could be going there for a multitude of business reasons. But something told her he was far too determined to drop his plans, and it was his intention to persuade the owners of the Alden place to sell up.

She stared at the empty street, knowing with a dread sense of inevitability that he'd be back.

ON AND OFF for the next few days, she worried, furtively peering out of the window before she went to work, looking over her shoulder all the time like a fugitive—or a criminal—and slowly her resentment grew that she, innocent and law-abiding, should feel unable to walk freely in her own hometown.

She'd said nothing to her grandfather when he'd telephoned. He had enough troubles of his own with the dispiriting news that there had been no interest in the garage at all. There was a chance that they might sell it before Giovanni bought the derelict site next door. A slim hope, but enough to renew her energies in coaxing the realtor to push its attractions.

They needed the money badly. Giovanni could sweep around the world making money hand over fist, but good men like her grandfather were finding it a struggle just to make ends meet and could only afford a much-needed holiday because the Rotary had come up trumps.

Dan Murphy was even too Irish-proud to let her parents know how things were. "Are you crazy?" he'd protested when she'd hesitantly suggested a few weeks ago that they tell her parents how difficult things were. "My aim is to sell up, buy a place with a garden and boast about it to your mother and father! They're working themselves silly out there in Puerto Rico, and I want them to come home for good soon—but only when there's something for them to come home *to*." He'd paused to tousle her hair fondly. "I'm too proud, sweetheart, to ask my own son for help. The children in his school need help more than we do." With a heaving sigh, he'd added, "It's not surprising you have a caring nature, with parents who give their last dollar to the poor and squander their fare home on buying toys and shoes for kids!"

Tina had smiled affectionately and hugged him, knowing he'd do the same. And often did. "You're a big softie, too," she'd said warmly. "And I love you. We'll be okay, I know it."

But she was worried. Giovanni could make life impossible if he insisted on seeing his mother. By Friday, Tina had begun to hope that Giovanni had been bluffing and was unable to face the painful meeting. He might even have canceled his deal to buy the Tamblyn house. She didn't dare ask. She might learn he was moving in next week.

After putting on her most sunshiny yellow halter dress and racing around doing the chores, she flew out of the apartment, did her normal check for a lurking blond guy, and jumped into her car. Another day, another frown line, she thought ruefully.

But she brightened, remembering that she'd managed to coax Ethan Bertelli—a member of the Terminators, a teenage gang that had caused so much trouble a while ago—to accept some novels from the dozens she'd bought at the library sale. There was hope for him yet, she thought, beginning to sing happily, her spirits raised.

Ethan had known a truckload of troubles, what with his spendthrift older brother, Glen, following in his father's footsteps and his mother's neglect. Mrs. Bertelli had shocked the Kowalski family next door with her drinking. Ethan had had little chance of going straight, but he was trying hard at last and she was glad.

Life wasn't so bad, she thought. People loved her. Optimism triumphed over her fears as she told herself that she'd cope. If she could cope with her lover killing Sue and little Michael, she could cope with anything.

The low-rise school building came up on her left, and she pulled into the parking lot, greeting students all-round as she strode enthusiastically into the building.

"'Morning, everyone!" she said cheerfully, entering the office door.

"My, you look bright and rarin' to go," commented her new secretary, eyeing the searingly bright yellow dress with obvious disapproval.

"It's summer," she said gently to him. "Rules get relaxed. All the students are in shorts and T-shirts. I'm not a teacher. I have to be approachable." Tina kept her smile going, remembering he had fixed ideas on women in the workplace, and felt sad that he was so uptight. "I'm open for business. Don't turn anyone away, will you?"

Happily she opened her door and firmly shut it on his tight face, delighted as always to be in her own room and not out in the soulless open office. She'd fought hard for somewhere to talk privately to the students, for a place to make homey and welcoming. Gazing around at the cozy, friendly chaos, she pushed aside some of the files on her desk and set about arranging the roses and pinks she'd bought from Juliana Van Bassen's flower shop after school yesterday.

The door opened and she turned, a happy smile on her face, expecting to see a student who needed her.

"It said Walk In," drawled Giovanni, "so I did."

CHAPTER SIX

TINA CONTROLLED the sudden lurch of her heart and turned a calm face to the mocking Giovanni. "Since you're obviously in an obedient mood, you can obey me and walk out," she said. He showed no sign of distress, his expression suave and smooth as though life were just fine. "I haven't time for arguing."

"There you go again, jumping to conclusions without all the evidence," he said with a theatrical sigh. Tina bristled, but her eyes were opening wider and wider at his choice of clothes. A silver-gray suit with a fine pink stripe, and a rose pink shirt with a light gray tie. No one else in the world could have worn that and looked good enough to eat, she marveled. "I've been talking to your principal and he sent me here for counseling," he said idly.

She lifted ironic eyebrows. "I'm flattered by his confidence in me. But you're beyond even my capabilities."

"Perhaps I am," he admitted. "I'd like to think so." He gave her a faintly amused smile. "By the way, I was a little disconcerted to find your door plastered with cartoons about cats. Didn't seem professional at all."

"On the contrary, it shows how warm and friendly I am," she said firmly, "though only toward those who deserve that kind of response," she added, in case he got the wrong idea. And because her pride was hurt by his gibe about her professionalism, she explained what had happened. "The students cut the cartoons out for me to cheer me up. My cat died, and one of them put up a photo of him. It sort of snowballed from there."

NO COST! NO OBLIGATION TO BUY!
NO PURCHASE NECESSARY!

PLAY "LUCKY 7" AND GET FIVE FREE GIFT

HOW TO PLAY:

1. With a coin, carefully scratch off the silver box at the right. Then check the claim chart to see what we have for you—FREE BOOKS and a gift—ALL YOURS! ALL FREE!

2. Send back this card and you'll receive brand-new Harlequin Presents® novels. These books have a cover price of $2.99 each, but they are yours to keep absolutely free.

3. There's no catch. You're under no obligation to buy anything. We charge nothing—ZERO—for your first shipment. And you don't have to make any minimum number of purchases—not even one!

4. The fact is thousands of readers enjoy receiving books by mail from the Harlequin Reader Service®. They like the convenience of home delivery . . . they like getting the best new novels months before they're available in stores . . . and they love our discount prices!

5. We hope that after receiving your free books you'll want to remain a subscriber. But the choice is yours—to continue or cancel, anytime at all! So why not take us up on our invitation, with no risk of any kind. You'll be glad you did!

You'll look like a million dollars when you wear this lovely necklace! Its cobra-link chain is a generous 18" long, and the multi-faceted Austrian crystal sparkles like a diamond!

PLAY "LUCKY 7"

**Just scratch off the silver box with a coin.
Then check below to see the gifts you get.**

YES! I have scratched off the silver box. Please send me all the gifts for which I qualify. I understand I am under no obligation to purchase any books, as explained on the back and on the opposite page.

106 CIH AQWL
(U-H-P-10/94)

NAME

ADDRESS   APT.

CITY   STATE   ZIP

7 7 7	**WORTH FOUR FREE BOOKS PLUS A FREE CRYSTAL PENDANT NECKLACE**
🍒 🍒 🍒	**WORTH THREE FREE BOOKS**
⬤ ⬤ ⬤	**WORTH TWO FREE BOOKS**
🔔 🔔 🍒	**WORTH ONE FREE BOOK**

THE HARLEQUIN READER SERVICE®: HERE'S HOW IT WORKS

Accepting free books places you under no obligation to buy anything. You may keep the books and gift and return the shipping statement marked "cancel". If you do not cancel, about a month later we'll send you 6 additional novels, and bill you just $2.44 each plus 25¢ delivery and applicable sales tax, if any.* That's the complete price, and—compared to cover prices of $2.99 each—quite a bargain! You may cancel at any time, but if you choose to continue, every month we'll send you 6 more books, which you may either purchase at the discount price...or return at our expense and cancel your subscription.

*Terms and prices subject to change without notice. Sales tax applicable in N.Y.

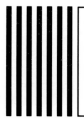

"Things do." He nodded sagely, his eyes dark and re-proachful. "Sometimes the snowball gets so big and suffo-cating that people forget how it started, and it rolls on, gathering more and more snow, covering up what should be—"

"You want me to counsel you on snowballs?" she inter-rupted curtly, well aware of his meaning. "I'm very busy. Try Highways."

"Your principal spoke well of you." Giovanni studied the large board of photos that ex-students had sent to her from all around the world, and then he moved on to the post-cards that covered the whole of one wall. He picked one off, read it and pinned it up again while she sneaked a chance to admire the width of his shoulders and back before he turned, caught her ogling and smiled at her disarmingly. "You have fans!"

Her chin came up. "I like the students, Gio. They like me."

"So it seems. You've built up a good reputation. Peo-ple's eyes light up when your name is mentioned," he said casually.

"That's nice," she said, wondering why he'd been men-tioning her name to anyone at all.

"It is. I'm relying on your being respected and valued," he said smoothly.

Worried, Tina shot him a glance from under her lashes. "Why?"

"I have several teenage cousins scattered around the States. Some of them are studying, some training for busi-ness," he said, sitting on the edge of her desk.

"That's nice." Showing great indifference, she dragged files and papers out from under him on the pretense of ex-amining them, but secretly was intensely curious to know what he was planning.

"I will help them to learn the auto trade from the bottom up," Giovanni said casually. "As I open more branches they can train for management."

"Nepotism," she suggested dryly. But she was tense. More branches. Which? Where? she thought in agitation.

"Call it what you like," he said with a shrug. "In Sicily we stick together. We all have a vested interest in each other's success. Why give a stranger a job when you can find someone in your family who's equally qualified?"

"It's a novel way of looking at it," she said, not sure how she felt about the practice. "I think you might be breaking a few laws...."

"I run a family business. That means I employ family. Now the situation is this. These school-age cousins have come from poor backgrounds...."

"Oh? You haven't helped them by putting your hand in your pocket, then," she said in chilling reproof.

He gave her a crucifying glare. "Don't ever question my loyalty and affection for my family," he said tightly. "And bear in mind that you don't give charity to a Sicilian. They are people of honor." She didn't dare make any comment on that, for his expression was lethal. But she hoped her eyes were telling him that in her opinion he didn't fit into that category. "Relatives who apply to me or my company get offered work—or assistance with educational grants," he said. "Satisfied?"

"I don't understand why you're telling me this." She frowned, finding to her irritation that she was stupidly rechecking the college placements she'd already completed.

"Because I'm interested in their welfare. I came to see the school some of them will attend and to meet their counselor."

"Here? In Eternity High?" she cried, aghast. Her arm jerked and nearly knocked over the flowers, but Giovanni caught them and stood them at a safer distance. He himself wasn't at any safe distance at all now, his body leaning very near, his hands supporting his weight. Their breaths mingled and she pressed her spine hard against the back of the chair because he looked far too sexy for so early in the morning.

"Eternity High is the neighborhood school. It's near to my house and I can keep an eye on them," he said with elaborate patience, his eyes homing in on the swell of flesh above her scoop neckline. "I promised their mothers."

"Near...near to you!" she repeated shakily and dragged her wits together again. He *was* intending to stay. She let out a low groan.

"Does that make your heart beat faster?" he murmured. "Does it unnerve you that I intend to get my own way in everything I've planned? It's taken me this long to get as rich as I need to be, and I'm going to hit this town like a whirlwind. I'll get planning permission for everything I want. The garage, the gas station, everything."

She'd been right! "You...did see the owners of the Alden place, then!" She felt a slow sinking of her stomach and all her hopes for her grandfather's comfortable retirement.

"Of course. You never doubted that I would, did you?"

Numbly Tina shook her head. Whatever claims she'd made earlier, somehow she doubted that the selectmen would hold Giovanni's imprisonment for manslaughter against him. He'd served his sentence and it had been an accident. Still...

"The selectmen have known Grandpa for years," she said proudly. "And he's well liked in the town. If there's a town meeting, he'd be supported in preference to you. The people of Eternity will think twice before—"

"I've spoken to each and every one of the selectmen. Without exception, they frowned and shook their heads when I posed my idea to them," he said with surprising honesty. "So I told them I was a resident, set out my plans, talked about improvements and prosperity and cleaning up that part of town."

"And?" she asked sullenly.

"Several were swayed by my eloquence," he said modestly.

She'd be tempted, too, she thought. "And the others?"

"Had reservations. So I offered them something."

"Don't tell me they took a bribe!" she scorned. "Never in a million—"

"About a million," he said solemnly. "I offered them a youth center and got the red-carpet treatment." He grinned crookedly. "Subject to the town meeting, I'm sure it'll go through, and then the way will be clear for my garage development. Incidentally, your principal nearly dropped his jaw on his desk he was so overwhelmed by the idea of a youth center. He sent his secretary out for chocolate cookies to celebrate. And he said *you'd* be thrilled to know that the students would have somewhere to let off steam and that would keep them busy in the evenings. You are thrilled, aren't you?" he murmured with a sweet smile.

"Oh, you bastard!" she breathed. "You utter bastard! You sneaky—"

"Careful," he warned in a hurt voice. "Mustn't annoy Mr. Generous Guy. You must think of the welfare of the young people in this community. They'd be horrified to learn you'd jeopardized their chances of a youth center. Your name would be mud, wouldn't it?"

Tina closed her eyes to hide the glistening tears. He was here to stay. And he'd heave Grandpa, Adriana and herself into a life of hell. In a rush of frustration and anger, she said, "I hope you rot in Hades!"

Giovanni slid off the desk and leaned forward. Suddenly she found herself flying backward in the chair toward the opposite wall, thrust there by a brief contemptuous hand that was as hard and as forceful as a falling rock. Giovanni grabbed both arms of the chair, stopping it before it actually crashed against the thin partition.

Tense from the knowledge that his straddled legs were clamped on either side of hers, Tina glared up at his brooding face and tried not to be so highly aware of the warmth of his body and its effortless projection of sexual menace. She could call for help. She ought to—

"Don't even think it," he said softly. "Not till you know what will happen if you show any opposition to me. If you won't do as I tell you—or if I find any difficulty in developing the Alden place—I will sell it to a rival in the garage business. Your grandfather would still be ruined. That's my kind of justice. If I lose, your grandfather—and you—lose. That's the first blow I'd strike."

Her grandfather's ruination! Her teeth clenched in anger. "And the second?" she asked, sounding miraculously calm. Somehow she was dredging up the control she'd shown when Glen Bertelli had threatened her with a knife if she didn't stop preaching sunshine and light to his brother Ethan.

There was a flash of admiration on Giovanni's face. "I'd rely on the efficacy of small-town gossip. Fan it a little by not denying any of those rumors about our past relationship," he said evenly. "Plenty flew around at the time and people's memories are long."

"You wouldn't!" She felt rising panic. The rumors had arisen after Gio's indictment, when people had discussed his intense passion and had embroidered a few stories of their own. She cringed, embarrassed now to recall them and the whispering groups of students gathered around Beth, discussing to Tina's horror her alleged larks in the school showers with Gio, nude bathing at midnight and . . .

Her face turned scarlet as she saw the sultry softness of Gio's mouth, the whiteness of his teeth parted in a feral smile as though he was thinking along the same lines—especially about the more outrageous sexual claims made about their relationship.

"Lies!" she grated.

"Originating from Beth," he said quietly. "She's prone to lying, as I hope you'll find out. And I hope for your sake that some of the more scurrilous stories don't emerge. It would look bad for you in your job."

"You know we didn't do those things! We might have been passionate but—" She stopped. Too many visions crowded her mind. His eyes flickered lazily as though the real memories were doing the same things to him as they were to her. Those memories, the intensity of the sex, the power of their love, the power of their laughter . . . She groaned, pained by her own gluttony, by the fun they'd shared. By shame.

"So. You'd like to forget what we did share," he said thickly.

"Yes!" she said fervently, her eyes ablaze. "It was an episode I never want to repeat. Everyone does something they're ashamed of. Behaving..." She bit her lip. "Being..."

"Wanton?" he suggested. "We needed each other so badly...."

Yes, yes! she wanted to cry. But instead, she gulped back the bittersweet taste in her mouth and tried to breathe less raggedly. "Being encouraged to experiment by a sexual athlete with the morals of a raccoon!" she grated.

He smiled, his mouth infinitely—unfairly—appealing. "Perhaps for my sanity I ought to forget what happened between us, as well," he said softly. "But have no doubt, Tina. When push comes to shove, I'd not deny any rumors. That wouldn't suit my purpose."

In his dark eyes was an excitement that electrified her. She felt the muscles in his thighs tighten their hold on her slender legs, the great charge of adrenaline that rushed through him, finding its way to her, too.

A shuddery breath shimmied from her lips and across his mouth. Helplessly she watched him breathe it in, enjoying it. "That would be brutal! I—I thought you were always honorable toward women?"

"Sicilian vengeance is always apt and too complex for others to understand. I haven't finished."

Was there more? she wondered hopelessly. "Then tell me the the the third part of this blackmail," she said coldly.

Giovanni flinched and his expression hardened. "It naturally involves my mother. Whatever happens to me, wherever I go, I would get to see her. You can't keep her locked up for the rest of her life. And I'd wait for the right moment, even if it took years, and then snatch her away and take her to live with me because once I decide what I want, nothing stops me from getting it. *Nothing.*"

"You swine! You'd put your mother through hell...!"
she began, almost spitting with fury, her hands clawing at
the arms of the chair.

"It would be your fault if I did," he growled softly. "Because abducting her is really quite an extreme action and you
can so easily prevent it."

This was it. Some ruthless plan to humiliate her—when
she was on her knees from his blows already. "Go on," she
muttered.

"I want my mother's love and I want to live here. You are
the whole key to my chance of achieving that. You can make
it happen," he told her quietly. "You know how to talk to
people. You can bring them around to behaving reasonably
and to take the balanced view. People admire and respect
you. They value your judgment. I want you to put your talents to work for me. I want you to put your whole heart and
soul into persuading everyone that I am decent, kind to an-
imals, trustworthy and bursting with honorable intentions." He straightened, but the compelling power of his
glittering eyes prevented her from moving an inch.

"You want a miracle!" she said scornfully. "If you think
I'm lying through my teeth..."

"Slowly and surely I *will* get back the respect I lost. You
will contribute in a way that is unique and that suits my idea
of poetic justice."

"And how will I make this contribution to your welfare?" she asked scathingly.

He laughed, but it was soft and sinister and chilled her to
the bone.

"By falling in love with me," he answered huskily.

Tina opened her mouth to gape at his intent face, initially dumbfounded by his sheer gall and then feeling that
familiar void inside her. She had never lost her love for him.
It was as fierce and as destructive as ever. And she must keep
it buried for her own good.

As she drew in a deep breath, ready to shower him in
scorn, she heard the door opening, saw Giovanni's narrowed eyes as he recognized the sound, too, and then he'd

bent to kiss her fiercely. She was so startled she did nothing.

"Oh! Excuse me!" came her secretary's disapproving voice. The door slammed shut.

The angry Tina pushed Giovanni's arms away, but he was already moving back, a look of satisfaction on his face. "You plague-ridden rat!" she breathed, hurling a cat ornament at him in sheer temper.

He caught it and returned it carefully to her desk, laughing in triumph. "It has begun," he said. "The gossip starts here."

Appalled, she stared at him, seeing her precious life being ruined by a vindictive, evil-minded avenger who was intent on breaking her heart. "Giovanni," she grated, lying to save her skin, "I couldn't fall in love with you even if my life depended on it!"

"Oh, it would only be pretend," he reassured her blandly. "We've already sown the seeds of our relationship."

"What do you mean?" she asked indignantly.

"For a start, our banter at the garage while the students looked on," he said with a satisfied air. "And the ice-cream act." He smiled a slow hungry smile. "One day I'll hold you to your promise to pour some over my naked body."

"I never said that!" she gasped, red with embarrassment.

"It's an experience I'm eager to try, nevertheless. I suppose it doesn't *have* to be you."

"It won't be!" she snapped, furious that jealousy should have made her wince so obviously.

"Well we must preserve the illusion that you'd like nothing better," he said silkily. "We were lovers once. What could be more natural," he murmured, "than for us to become lovers again? Folks here would be talking, wondering, expecting fireworks to fly between us, anyway."

It was too cruel. She pressed her fingers to her temples where her veins pulsed. Lovers again... Terrible needs swept through her—for their love to be true, to be in his arms every day, cherished, held by him. And he was asking her to *pretend!*

"I'd disenchant them if they gossiped. I'd put a halt to any connection between us...." she began wildly.

"I don't think you would," he said silkily. "I doubt you'd want to."

"What...what do you mean?" she demanded hotly. Had he found her out? Did he know? she wondered guiltily. She hated him—because she loved him and knew only a suicidal maniac would let herself love Giovanni.

Thoughtfully, his eyes holding hers prisoner, he touched her, and in that touch, in that look, was her downfall. She wanted to pretend. Yearned to play out her long-suppressed emotions, to give them freedom and perhaps be free of them in time. Her huge eyes grew softer, wider, limpid with longing, and he smiled.

"I can ruin your grandfather. I can ruin you in several ways," he said, with a soft callousness that took her breath away. "We ought to legitimize our recent clinch, or the whispers will suggest you often kiss men in your office."

"No, Gio!" she protested. "You—"

"If we're clever," he went on, "that kiss your secretary interrupted can be turned into an embrace between two people who've just made a commitment to one another."

"I won't let people think I'm your mistress!" she gasped.

"That's not what I'm suggesting," he drawled. "Our relationship must be above reproach. It must be love of the highest kind."

If only! she thought bitterly. "Why would you want our relationship to be pure and noble? It doesn't sound like you at all."

His eyes glittered. "You still don't get it, do you?" he murmured. "My close association with you will remove any barriers people have put up against me. If you, the sister of the woman who died in the collision with my car, can forgive and forget sufficiently to become my wife, then they must wipe it from their minds, too, and treat me like a normal, decent human being."

Tina felt the heartbreak tearing through her body as she stared at him, wide-eyed and quivering. "Your...wife?" she gulped in bewilderment, a thousand levers clicking in her brain and making it whirl crazily.

"Just pretend. We won't go through with it," he reminded her consolingly.

"You can bet your sweet life we won't!" she said raggedly, her eyes dark with pain.

"I will be seen as courteous and gentlemanly, earnestly doing my best to clear my name. And you will be supporting me in this—"

"No! Never!" she cried, refusing to go along with his horrible plan.

"But you will," he insisted softly. "Gradually, over a period of time, you'll get my mother used to the idea that I'm here to stay and that she's mistaken about me. You could do that, but only you, because she trusts you and has always loved you," he said with surprising tenderness. "Gently you will persuade her that you love me, that it would be your greatest joy to see us reconciled."

"No, no!" she whispered in horror. "I can't lie to her!"

"Lie?" he queried, and she stiffened. But her attention was diverted when he absently stroked the soft material of her dress where it lay folded over her thigh, and after a moment of delicious enjoyment, she slapped his hand away. "I will be allowed to do that when we are engaged."

"I can't!" she croaked.

"Persuade my mother," he murmured. "Tell her of the things we do together, the meals we eat, how we hold hands—"

"Gio, please!" she protested weakly, shaking her head.

"Tell her of the fun we have together," he said ruthlessly. "How we laugh at the same things, enjoy the same activities, that you feel I am the most wonderful— Something wrong, Tina?" he asked, in low, darkly throbbing tones.

"You know I can't do those things with you," she muttered miserably. "Those days are long gone." To her eternal sorrow.

"I don't think you have any choice," he answered mildly. "Of course, it would be in your best interest to get my mother's mind changed as quickly as possible. We'd have to stay engaged, you see, till she came to live with me. Once she's settled, we can break off our engagement and remain—apparently—good friends. How's that?"

"Gruesome," she muttered, flushing when he laughed. "You get everything you want if I agree," she complained. "Your mother's affection, the Tamblyn house, the acceptance of the town *and* the Alden place. I get nothing."

His mouth twitched. "I think you might be surprised how much you get."

"Don't think I'd let you make love to me!" she cried hotly.

"It would be your decision how far you played your part," he answered seriously, but his eyes told her that he expected her to succumb, and she wasn't sure what she might do if she was continually in his company. "You'd get a good sale on the garage—I can arrange that. Your grandfather can retire on the proceeds, and you'd have somewhere better to live. You'd have total access to my mother, who'd be deliriously happy, I promise you. Your students would have a youth center. Not a bad trade-off, considering the alternatives."

Feeling quite weak, she leaned back in the chair in defeat. Help him or suffer the consequences. Life would be unbearable either way. "I can't."

"Your grandfather is frail. I chatted to your part-timers," he said quietly. "He's killing himself with worry, with working harder than he should, with trying to provide for you and Adriana while the nurse's bills mount up. Inch by inch, he's dying, Tina. You can prevent that if you love him."

"Of *course* I love him!" she whispered, her heart aching for her brave grandfather. "I—I don't know if I can pre-

tend we're in love,'' she mumbled. How could she when i
was true? And to hold back, to stop him using her as a sex
ual release, would be virtually impossible since she wante
the feel of his arms around her so much.

"Stand up." Giovanni's order was so authoritative tha
she found herself on her feet before she realized. Crushe
against his body. Kissed stupid, dizzy with kisses, unable t
breathe, to think, to protest.... With a show of reluctance
he lifted his mouth from hers and leaned back to see her re
action.

Slowly her eyes opened. Her lips were still open in a de
manding pout. "I hate you!" she said, coming to her sense
and deliberately drawing the back of her hand across he
mouth.

"But you don't find it hard to show sexual willingness,'
he pointed out cruelly. "Tina, we can operate on that leve
so we can fool a few people that we're united in every othe
way." He smiled mockingly at her flushed face. "We botl
want things resolved fast. So let's go for it—and let's lool
on it as a bit of fun."

"Fun!" A knock on the door interrupted her intende
tirade. "Come in!" she called in relief.

The door opened slowly and she blushed guiltily, won
dering if she looked as disheveled and ravished as she felt
It was Ethan Bertelli, peering around the door and lookin,
uncertain about coming in at all.

Dear Ethan, she thought fondly, pulling herself together
He'd broken the spell that Giovanni had woven around her
"Hi, Ethan," she said warmly. "I've got those books fo
you. Come and help me look. What a mess this place is!"
She sighed, chattering on in her nervousness. "This i
Giovanni—"

"Yeah, the guy with the Lamborghini!" enthused Ethar
suddenly, shaking Giovanni by the hand. "'Morning, sir!'

Tina continued to search for Ethan's books while he and
Gio chatted about the crowd-stopping car. Absently she hal
listened to the conversation. Gio was good with Ethan, no
questioning or criticizing some of his wilder claims and no

showing disapproval when Ethan boasted unrealistically about the speed he could get out of his own car. It was a chat between equals, and she pretended *not* to find the books for some time because Ethan was opening up and relaxing, quieting down and sounding more normal, shooting less of a line than usual. He was a nice guy underneath, she thought fondly. Ethan, of course.

"Well, ain't this cozy!"

Tina's head jerked round at the harsh sound of Glen Bertelli's voice. "Hello, Glen," she said pleasantly. Behind him stood Jim Falconer—twenty-one and unemployed like Glen, but utterly evil. "Ethan's just—"

Glen glowered at Ethan, his lip-chewing brother. "I told you to stay clear of this reforming—"

He used a derogatory four-letter word that made Tina gasp in shock. And then Glen was gasping himself, fighting for breath, as he was lifted clear off his feet by the fast-moving and unbelievably incensed Giovanni.

"Apologize to the lady and then get the hell out before I separate your mouth from your face!" Giovanni snarled.

"Leave him alone!" Ethan pleaded.

"Sorry!" squeaked Glen.

There was a scuffle as Jim tried to wade in, but Giovanni's superior bulk and strength, combined with an intelligent use of leverage, forced the two young men past the riveted office staff until all Tina could hear was the sound of swing doors banging together, raised voices and then the crunch of tires on the gravel.

Ethan ran out and Tina groaned. He'd never dare to speak to her again. She glowered when Giovanni came into the room, dusting off his hands. He looked totally unmarked, which was unusual for someone who tangled with Glen and Jim.

"Thanks a lot," she muttered sarcastically.

"Don't you like being protected?" asked Giovanni in surprise.

"I could have handled that," she replied shortly.

"I'm sure you could have," he agreed. "But I can't stand by and do nothing when someone insults you."

Tina lowered her eyes. Strangely she felt flattered. Cherished and feminine. It was rather nice and he'd shown a good side of himself for a change. "You can't?" she asked uncertainly.

"No. How would it look if your lover doesn't defend you? You've got to *think* of these things, Tina."

"Oh!" she said furiously. "You swine!" He'd clamped a hand over her mouth, and the word "swine" was smothered.

"Quietly," he said, holding her a prisoner as she wriggled in frustration. "We can't let them think we're arguing. You're grateful to me for defending your honor, remember?" He gave a wicked grin. "You didn't think I was doing that because I had a high regard for you, do you?" he murmured. "That would be the mark of a guy who cared about you, wouldn't it?"

"Mmm!" she growled beneath his hand.

"I'll let you go when you've calmed down," he said, sounding inordinately pleased with himself. "And when you've agreed to my terms. I want your wholehearted cooperation in this." His eyes gleamed. "We behave like lovers. Some passion would be natural. Nothing too hot, mind. I want a decent reputation. Thus the world smiles on us both, and some of your Miss Wonderful character rubs off on me. Nod your head when you agree."

Her mutinous eyes sparkled with razor-blade lights, and he laughed, the sound going through her like a hot knife through butter. Melting her on the way. His arm swept farther around her body and he bent her back farther and farther till she almost lost her balance.

"Refuse and I will persuade you by kissing you—here," he murmured, touching his lips to her collarbone. "And here—" his face nuzzled the neckline of her dress, pushing it down an inch "—and here." Wrapped in shameful delight, she savored the soft drift of his mouth along the warm satin on either side of her cleavage and ineffectually moaned her protest while his kisses became more fevered, more passionate than ever. "Here, here and here," he said huskily. "Are you ready to agree yet?"

Someone might come in, she thought hazily. As the morning drew on, her room was always like the Boston tunnel during rush hour, with people and calls coming in at her from every which way. And Giovanni's mouth had reached the dip between her breasts, his hand creeping down to her rear.

She couldn't resist. She had to. He'd seduce her here and now.... But to be his intended bride... Weakness was invading her mind and her body. She wanted him. She hated him. *Agree,* her mind screamed. *Find a way to back out later! Refuse and...*

"Tina," he whispered, his voice thick with passion. And there was the iron hardness of his body heating her loins, demanding her submission.

Panicked, she nodded. "Mmm!" she mumbled in despair. His palm tasted warm and she had a dreadful desire to kiss it, but the pressure over her mouth was lifted. He released her completely, as though he'd only bothered to assault her to achieve his purpose.

Not, she thought crossly, smoothing down her dress and sullenly checking her hair with shaking hands, because she was wildly irresistible. Peeved, she began the slow process of gathering herself together while he watched in silence. He thought he could achieve everything he wanted. Nothing shook his equilibrium, not even a warm curvy woman in his arms, while she quivered and ached and was a total mess. It would serve him right if—

"Walk out with me to the car."

Tina looked up at his command and eyed his hand rebelliously. "What for?"

"Effect," he replied. "What the hell do you think?"

For a second or two she studied him, his cynical expression and indifference denting her pride. Every other guy who'd kissed her had been enthusiastic. Every other man who'd gone out with her had been keen to repeat the experience. Not Giovanni. He remained immune.

How satisfying if—

"Okay," she said. "Let me get my face right." Feeling deprived and resentful, she tried out a simper and he grinned, so she changed that and revealed what lay behind her dislike—a powerful, deeply carnal desire.

His grin faded to uncertainty. "A little strong," he said, then had to clear his throat. "Something in between?"

Encouraged by the rough passion in his voice, she throttled back a little. "We'll fool them all," she said, taking his proffered hand. *And I'll fool you,* she told herself grimly as he opened the door for her and she saw the expectant eyes of all the office staff whip in their direction. He'd get more than he bargained for.

"Pick you up after school, then, darling," Giovanni said to her fondly. "We'll go and choose the—" He checked himself, gave her a conspiratorial look and muttered, *"The ring!"* in a whisper loud enough to have reached across a baseball field.

Tina tried to ignore the gasps and flutterings going on all around her, and did her best to concentrate on looking soppily into Giovanni's eyes in the way any love-struck woman should. "How wonderful!" she said, squeezing his hand.

"Darling!" he breathed, stumbling into a desk. "Oh!" He grinned sheepishly. "Sorry! Rather dazed!" he explained.

Brilliant, mused Tina. He seemed utterly confused and glowing with happiness. Rat! She knew the smooth suave Giovanni would never lose his sense of dignity sufficiently to bump into anything. What an actor he was!

"He will *not* wear his glasses! Aren't men vain?" Tina said with a smile to anyone listening. Which was virtually everyone. Under a battery of astonished eyes, she and Giovanni giggled their way around the rest of the obstacles, and Giovanni tenderly helped her through the swing doors with the most unctuous smile she'd ever seen.

"Now say goodbye nicely," he murmured, a rather unsettling gleam in his eye.

"Goodbye nice—" Her planned reply was smothered in a blatant piece of theater, with Giovanni whirling her into his arms, bending her back like a tango dancer's partner in a thirties' movie and pressing an enthusiastic kiss on her startled mouth. To which she obligingly responded till common sense triumphed. "Gio!" she mumbled, as he dizzily swung her upright again. "That wasn't—"

"Decent. I know," he said with a disarmingly apologetic smile for the benefit, she knew, of the goggle-eyed staff members pressing their noses to the nearby window. "But that was instead of a smack on the hand for suggesting I needed glasses. You mustn't play those kinds of games with me, Tina. You'll get badly hurt. As for the kiss, it's clear to everyone that you have just made me—" he licked his lips as if they were dry "—the happiest man in the world," he said a little hoarsely, "and I do have the excuse of hot Mediterranean blood...."

"Which you'll find flowing all over the parking lot if you do that again!" she said, smiling with the same level of sweetness as she judged any embarrassed and newly engaged counselor should. "That's another thing, *darling*," she said, flapping her lashes prettily at him and being rewarded by his genuine amusement. "Isn't our engagement a teensy bit sudden and unbelievable?"

"We were in love once, weren't we?"

"No."

He grinned at her bitter reply and tousled her hair affectionately. "I'm a man in a hurry."

Her eyes chilled. "Grandpa and Adriana will come home to a shock I don't want either of them to have," she said anxiously.

"You've time to find the best way to tell them," he replied. "To look starry-eyed and happy, to tell them you've fallen madly, hopelessly in love with the most wonderful guy in the world. They love you. They'll be pleased."

"You really do think on the run, don't you?" she said grudgingly.

"I have to. I've got a lot of time to make up. See you. Wave me off and do that simpering smile. It's a real killer."

Tina heaved a deep breath and made her eyes go soft and adoring. He thought he had her exactly where he wanted her. But he'd find out she could throw a few curves, too. Waving madly, a sweet and sickly smile on her face, she turned, eager to hatch plans to thwart him.

CHAPTER SEVEN

THERE WAS an excited buzz in the office when she came back, and she had to play coy, refusing to tell them anything. Since she had the mother of a truant waiting to see her, she was saved from any more explanations. She enthusiastically tackled the mother's complaint that her welfare checks had stopped and reminded the mother that they'd start coming again once the boy returned to school.

Little time came her way to think because inquiries, confirmations, worried students and the problems of retakes hurtled at her thick and fast. In addition, she managed to prevent a headstrong student from leaving home after a dispute about his career and made arrangements to be there for a family conference, discussed homework schedules with a martinet of a father, and listened to a thirteen-year-old girl's worries about her parents' divorce.

A normal day in the life of. Tiring, rewarding, frustrating. She'd have to hatch plans on the run, she thought wearily. And she was in no mood when school finished to see Giovanni waiting for her, talking to a crowd of students again.

Dressed in immaculate jeans and a casual green shirt, he was leaning nonchalantly against the passenger door of his car, and she felt envious of his evident interest in the students. He didn't treat her with as much courtesy or seriousness, she thought irritably.

"Gio!" she called.

"Tina!" Immediately he leapt forward, drawing her through the group around him and grinning his heart-stopping grin. "I've missed you, darling!" he whispered fervently, opening the passenger door for her.

Just the right amount of shake in his voice. Loving, but not weak. Clever brute! With hatred in her heart for his far-too-plausible act, she smiled up at him, thinking that his whispers were becoming famous.

"Have you? I must admit, I haven't had time. I've been rather busy," she said casually, as she maneuvered herself into the luxurious leather seat, implying she'd virtually forgotten him.

He bent to do the seat belt up for her, his face very close, his eyes dark with warning. "No putdowns!" he muttered. Then he straightened. "All set for the jewelers?" he said loudly. "Fancy underwear next—"

"Gio!" Tina blushed, furious with him. There had been a stifled intake of breath from a nearby student, and Tina was offended by what Giovanni was doing to her solid reputation. "Let's go," she said urgently.

His hand brushed her cheek. "Serves you right for saying you didn't miss me," he said, for her ears alone. "I can play these games better than you. I did warn you. Don't push your luck."

With a friendly wave to everyone, Giovanni flicked on the ignition. In an instant, the engine leapt into life, growling menacingly like some wild beast that had been temporarily harnessed. He eased his hips back into the deep seat and she felt a quick response fire her body, as if he had turned on some secret ignition inside her, as well.

"We ought to look as if we're chatting animatedly," he said, flashing her a toothy grin.

She whizzed one back at him. "What a nice car this is!" she said brightly as he hovered in one place for a while, deliberately affording a large number of curious students a good look at the two of them, smiling inanely. "It must be a pretty powerful machine," she said, listening to the purr of the engine. At least they were moving forward. Slowly. "I imagine," she said dryly, "it does go faster than a crawl?"

"One hundred and eighty miles an hour," he said softly, and pressed the accelerator gently to take them onto the open road. "I like the sense of being in control of such a beautiful powerful machine. She's lovely. A little wayward, a little hard to handle and potentially lethal. But I know exactly how to keep her in check and when to release the pressure and let her have her head. It's all a matter of timing and highly developed senses, you see. That and a strong hand."

Tina could feel the power there, waiting to escape and surge into life, and something wild caught hold of her, a desire to break free and allow her pent-up sexuality its head. But not with Giovanni, she mused, covertly watching the way he handled the car.

With ease. A natural confidence, born of long experience. So it would be with women—with her, if she allowed him to make love to her. He'd be too sure of himself and she'd think of all the women he'd taken in his experienced sex life—and the one he'd loved especially. She tightened her mouth unhappily.

Yet despite her rationalizing, she watched with dazed desire the way his hand caressed the wheel and lovingly stroked the gearshift with a brief sweep of his palm, and the atmosphere became tenser as the temperature inside the car went up.

Consequently she was a little shaky when he parked near the jewelry shop. Aware of this, he helped her out, every gesture of his body expressing love and desire. Or so it seemed, and she felt she couldn't go through with this, not with people she knew.

"Not here! Can't we get something in Boston?" she pleaded.

"The object is to publicize our relationship, not hide it," he drawled, then he switched on a smile of neon brilliance. "Sweet and tender. A little dazed. Got that? This has been a whirlwind decision and we're staggering from our reckless daring."

"You can say that again," she muttered darkly, as he enthusiastically rushed her into the store.

Alerted by the bell, a woman with honey blond hair popped up from behind the counter, and a warm smile spread over her face. "Tina! Hi!" she said in delight.

Tina managed to smile back, a little surprised to see Marion Kent working there, instead of her parents. "Marion, how nice to see you," she said uncertainly. And stopped bothering to hide her embarrassment, because Marion wasn't listening, anyway. She was staring at Gio in shock.

"Hello, Marion," murmured Giovanni, holding out his hand. "Remember me? Gio Kowalski. How are you?"

"I..." Marion looked anxiously at Tina for guidance on how to behave toward Giovanni.

"It's all right," he said softly, his arm around Tina affectionately. "The past is all over now. Tina and I have had a long talk, haven't we, darling?"

He gave her a warm squeeze and she fixed a smile on her face. "Yes, Marion," she said huskily. "Gio's coming back was a shock. This is as awkward for you as it is for me," she said with frank honesty. "We'll take it one step at a time, shall we?"

"Y-yes." Marion sounded perplexed, and Tina felt awful about putting her in such a difficult situation. It had been the newly married Marion and Geoff, along with her family and one or two other close friends, who'd helped her to cope with her ordeal in the witness box by ensuring she was never alone and never without comfort and support.

"Where are the babies?" Tina asked, moving to a subject guaranteed to take the apprehension from Marion's gentle eyes.

True to expectation, Marion smiled. "Out with the fond grandparents," she said happily. "I thought I'd put in a few hours and give my parents a break. They're running the shop now, but they're playing hookey for a while," explained Marion shyly.

"You have children?" asked Giovanni warmly. "How many? Boys? Girls?" Despite his interest, Tina sensed how stiff his body was and knew he was remembering his own recently dashed hopes.

"Twins!" said Marion proudly, and proceeded to give the fascinated Giovanni all the relevant details, producing photographs of the three-month-old babies for him to admire.

With growing concern, Tina watched him chatting to the usually reserved Marion, coaxing confidences from her with breathtaking ease. She discussed babies with the enthusiastic and apparently knowledgeable Giovanni, delightedly sharing information about disposable diapers and baby buggies and theories of routine versus flexibility.

Tina groaned to herself. Marion had obviously been swept up by his disarming manner and his interest in the children she'd waited so long to have. He seemed to understand her problems, and it was clear he'd been involved with his younger cousins in Sicily, taking an active part in the upbringing and entertaining of the many children in his extended family. Mr. Nice Guy. Very soon Tina would have to break that image somehow without jeopardizing her own position.

"You both must come for Sunday lunch and meet the babies," suggested Marion to Tina's horror.

"We'd like nothing better," said Giovanni, his eyes alight with pleasure. "The two of us! Thank you."

"Have you... have you come back to see your mother, Gio?" Marion asked gently.

"That's right." Giovanni smiled tenderly at the apprehensive Tina and gave her shoulders an apparently spontaneous hug. "And... Oh, darn it, Tina. I've got to tell someone. I'm fit to burst!" he said with an abashed laugh. "This is a secret to keep! I came back to Eternity for Tina. That's why we're here in your shop." His lopsided grin was utterly winsome. "We're—" Tina's eyes widened as the grin became more uncontrolled and ecstatic "—getting engaged!"

"That's wonderful!" cried Marion, hugging the tense Tina excitedly. "After what happened... it does my heart good to know things are okay between you two again. Tina did love you so much." Tina felt sick and trapped. She'd have to explain that one away too. "But isn't this a bit sudden?" added Marion.

"You call eight years sudden? Haven't you heard of letter writing and the telephone?" asked Giovanni. Marion nodded, exchanging a smiling glance with Tina who knew that Marion's own love life had first been conducted from a distance. "She kept quiet about it because, well, obviously it's a delicate situation," he explained, sounding the soul of tact. "We're looking for a ring. The best you have, the most special you can find."

"I'm thrilled." Marion smiled. "When's the wedding to be?"

"Soon," said Giovanni.

"Ages," said Tina at the same time. There was an awkward silence. "He's got no idea how much there is to do," explained Tina.

"I've got a book," he said earnestly, producing a pink paperback.

Tina stared at the cover in amazement. *"A Step-by-Step Checklist for the Happy Couple,"* she read in a strangled squeak.

"I picked up a leaflet about the services of Weddings, Inc., and the book was recommended, too," he said, and Tina worked hard to keep the smile on her face. Word would be getting around. There was nothing she could do, and she felt trapped by him in terrible lies. "Weddings, Inc., makes getting married so simple!" he went on enthusiastically. "And the book fills in everything else we need to know. Look, darling. All about ushers and guest lists and caterers—I've already seen Manuel, by the way, and he's bringing over menus. And I've bought a file-card system and a notebook to record gifts, as the book suggests. I thought we'd put the information on my computer, because it's pretty complicated. I know you're busy, but I can handle most of it."

"It seems you've done a good deal already," she said faintly, sick with the ghastly masquerade.

"Bear up, darling," he said tenderly. "I'm with you."

That was what she hated. The fact that he wasn't. She turned away with a quick nod of her head and pretended to look at the display of bracelets.

"I've never known a man so enthusiastic about his own wedding!" exclaimed Marion. "Look, Tina. What do you think of these?"

As she showed them a selection of her newest ring designs, Marion's face was alight with happiness for Tina, who found it hard to keep the lie going when Marion produced one of her most beautiful and expensive designs and Giovanni took the ring from its box and placed it reverently on her finger.

Tina stared hazily at the huge diamond surrounded by sapphires and couldn't help saying brokenly, "It's...it's lovely!"

"Diamonds for eternity, sapphires to match your eyes," Giovanni told her huskily, and Tina felt incapable of speech for a while because of the long slow look he gave her. Loving, wistful, yearning.

"Oh, Gio!" she whispered shakily, pleading with her eyes to be released from this torture.

"Tina!" he breathed, as though choked with emotion.

Somehow she managed to drop her gaze, her lashes wet with tears at the unbearable cruelty. Giovanni kissed each lowered lid, and she knew he tasted the salt because, for some reason, he gave her hand a compassionate and surreptitious squeeze of encouragement.

Knowing that Marion must be looking on, Tina took care to examine the ring. Her finger smoothed over the glittering facets of the diamond and traced the platinum leaves and flowers in which the stones were set. A ring to end all rings. And everything was a sham. She wanted to cry.

Heartbroken at the cruel irony of the situation, Tina tried to speak and only came out with a croak. "I...can't..."

"Don't worry about the price, darling. It's perfect. I don't care what it costs." His eyes gleamed and he said softly, "It's worth it."

Worth her humiliation and the achievement of all his dreams! After Marion excused herself to answer the telephone in the back room, Tina lifted her head bravely. "But—"

His finger pressed firmly on her soft coral mouth. "No *buts*. I want to give you what you deserve. I've dreamed of this," Giovanni murmured, gathering her in his arms. "I've thought of this moment for years. I..." He hesitated and she shot him a suspicious glance. His eyes looked soft and shiny, as though he, too, was upset. And...perhaps there was a hint of sorrow there, she thought, for the innocence he'd lost long ago. Her lip trembled and he touched it wonderingly with his finger again. "I've never stopped loving you," he said huskily. "Never." There was a long silence while their gazes meshed and she believed what he was saying. May the gods help her, she actually believed him. "Tina!" he whispered.

"No!" said Tina in distress. She wanted to get out. To run and never stop. She felt as though she'd been flung into a dark pit, her senses in a confused muddle as though she was on the verge of screaming, sobbing, laughing....

"Darling!" he whispered now.

His soft, warm and infinitely welcome mouth covered hers before she could protest again. It was such a tender gentle kiss, filled with such poignant loving, that she couldn't resist it. All her heart went into her response, all those emotions he'd aroused. Sentiment, forlorn hopes, the poignancy of the situation. All her love.

Her eyes closed in anguish. She loved him. He was inflicting pain on her and still she ached for him, to be loved by a flawed and damaged man.

For a few agonizing moments she allowed herself to enjoy his sweet caresses till her sorrowing heart reached the point of utter desolation. She wanted to be kissed by him. Why should she keep denying what was true?

Something made her hand reach up to his head, and she splayed her fingers in the silken blond hair, gripping the thick waves and forcing his mouth more firmly on hers. She felt his body tense and then he was responding with fire, whispering words of love into her ear and her softly gasping mouth.

"Oh, Gio!" she whispered helplessly, and allowed their tongues to touch.

Standing body to body with him, she felt the leap of his arousal, felt him suck in his stomach muscles in shock. Instinct told her that she must now push him away, but instead, he surprised her by putting her gently from him. She realized he had no intention of letting her believe he was in any danger of succumbing to her.

"That was a nice thank-you," he said huskily.

"Was it?" she murmured dazedly, wondering if that hot and ragged breathing she heard was his—or hers. Or maybe it came from them both.

"It deserves a proper response later," he said quietly. "When we're alone."

Her lashes fluttered up in sudden alarm to find that he was looking at her in a disturbing way. Never alone—not with him, she decided then and there. Safety in numbers. She'd surround herself with people and thwart his plans to seduce her and add her to his list of triumphs.

A spilling resentment pushed that decision to one side, clamoring to be heard. Be alone with Giovanni! it demanded. Be wrapped in his arms, kissed to a state of unheeding intoxication! Tina felt her eyes widen in astonishment. A wicked seduction was taking place. Not by Giovanni, but by her own greedy self!

Confused, she crossed to the window and pretended to be admiring the ring again. In reality she was trying to control her emotions. Desire, anger, fear. Oh, God! she thought, shaking like a leaf. She didn't know which was worse—going along with the deceit or the mortifying fact that she was enjoying their forced intimacy!

Meanwhile, Marion had returned, and Gio was chatting with her. "Marion, remember—this is a secret. We need about forty-eight hours before the news leaks," Giovanni was saying in a conspiratorial tone, and Tina smiled wryly.

If he hoped Marion would ignore his wishes and feel compelled to gossip, he'd picked the wrong outlet for their "secret." But Tina didn't know how many others he'd leaked the news to, prancing around and buying books on wedding etiquette and file cards! "We'll be calling Dan tonight," he confided.

Tina felt numb at the thought. The pebble had been thrown, the ripples were fanning out, and she was falling into the whirlpool he'd created. She shrank at the thought of explaining her decision to her grandfather. Somehow she had to persuade him she was serious—and she'd never deceived him in her life. He'd see through her for sure.

"And what about...?" The tactful and sensitive Marion went a little pink with embarrassment.

Tina smiled weakly. "Yes, Gio's mother. She'll be told gently," she said, knowing what Marion had hesitated to say. "We can't give her two shocks, one after the other." She twiddled the ring. It felt strange. "We... we have to get her used to the idea that Gio is back first, and then tell her we're engaged—very, very gently."

"I understand." Marion came forward and took Tina's hands in hers. "I'm so happy for you," she said quietly. "You've sacrificed so much for other people. It's time you had some joy of your own." She looked back at Giovanni. "Tina's a wonderful person. You must be a very special guy if she loves you. She deserves the best."

Tina saw that his smile was a little thin and that his eyes glittered as he lifted an expectant eyebrow at her. "He is...the best," she confirmed dutifully in a choky voice.

He'd once been, she thought sadly. Something dreadful had soured him. When he'd arrived from Sicily he'd been untainted and eager, full of enthusiasm and a fierce sense of justice and honor. It had never occurred to her that he'd so misuse his talents.

Perhaps seeing Beth's house had made him envious and overambitious. She imagined that was why Beth had told her he'd been so desperate to persuade her family to top up the scholarships he'd won as an investment in him, their future son-in-law. Without that extra money he couldn't cover all his tuition fees at Harvard. Hence the row with Beth that night when she refused to cooperate, the punches that had bruised her bony shoulders, the way he'd gripped her arms so hard that five purple smears had been left on each arm, which Beth had shown everyone in sight to prove what a bully the Golden Boy really was. Now Tina knew that to be a fact. He played to win. Hard, ruthlessly, without considering the risks or who was hurt.

But he'd met his match this time. He wouldn't achieve his dreams if she had anything to do with it!

Wretchedly she watched him pay the bill, and in accepting Marion's warm congratulations and good wishes, he managed to sound sheepish and proud at the same time. A nice guy. The sort you brought home to Mom.

This would happen frequently over the next few days, she told herself gloomily. He'd charm everyone around him by identifying whatever was important in their lives and showing an intense interest in it. Slowly and surely he'd quell any opposition because she, the woman he'd wronged in so many ways, "loved" him. And there was nothing she could do about it. He'd begin to lord it about the town and later, when they'd parted, he'd meet some woman, settle down....

She dug her nails into her palms, hating the idea. The ring caught the sun streaming into the shop and winked at her. Tina scowled back, her heart heavy that she should be involved so deeply in deception. It seemed amoral. You didn't fool around with love.

"Ready, darling?" Giovanni's arm came around her shoulders.

Tina shuddered and turned that into a sigh. "Yes!" she said brightly. "Bye Marion. Love to Geoff and the babies!"

Giovanni's crushing grip on her elbow and the pressure on her back urged her forward. With the new ring burning her finger, Tina walked to the car with him, wondering how she was going to help Adriana come to terms with her son's return. He drove her back to her car without speaking a word to her until she was ready to drive away.

"I'll pick you up for dinner at seven. By which time you'll have told your grandfather," he said curtly.

"I have something in the freezer, thanks," she said haughtily. "You don't have to buy me dinner just because—"

"I do, unfortunately," he muttered ungraciously. "We are 'secretly' engaged. I want the whole town to know about it. What would you do if we were really engaged?"

Dance. Tina blinked, surprised by the weird response her brain had come up with. "Get myself committed for insanity," she said tartly, thinking wryly that perhaps she ought to in any case.

His dark eyebrow twitched up. "Failing that?" he asked silkily.

"Find a good psychoanalyst."

"You'd go out to dinner with your beloved," drawled Giovanni, untouched by her sarcasm. "That's what we'll do. And if you don't want trouble for your grandfather, you'd better play the part of my delighted fiancée again. Can you find something that fits in with our celebration?"

"Black?" she suggested, thinking it would match the depression she'd feel, pretending to be engaged.

"Normally I'd say yes. But I want us to be noticed. I've booked a table in the center of the restaurant. Do you have anything suitably eye-catching?"

Tina lowered her eyes, thinking of her scarlet-woman dress. She'd bought it in a sale, dazzled by its wickedness, and had never dared to wear it. This was the moment.

He wanted eye-catching, he'd get eye-catching.

"I think I can come up with something," she said modestly, and managed to produce a sweet and innocent smile.

TINA TOOK a deep breath. She and her grandfather had exchanged inquiries about one another and Adriana, about the holiday and the weather. Now came the difficult part.

"Grandpa, this is going to come as a shock," she began hesitantly. "I didn't want to tell you on the phone, but I'm anxious you should hear it from me first."

"You're not ill, Tina?" he asked worriedly.

"No, no!" she assured him. And felt a deep hatred for Giovanni. She'd never done a deceitful thing in her life. "I'm . . . I'm engaged, Grandpa."

"You what? Who to?" he demanded in astonishment. "You weren't even dating anyone when we left!"

"I know!" she said, cradling the telephone receiver between shoulder and jaw, wrapped in her cozy toweling robe. She plucked at the frayed edges of the belt and avoided telling him it was Giovanni. She didn't want her grandfather to cut short his well-deserved holiday and come back before she'd sorted Giovanni out and sent him on his way. One mention of Gio's name and her grandfather would be packing suitcases.

Tina bit her lip. The green digital figures on her watch were telling her that she ought to have started this conversation an hour ago. In twenty-five minutes, Giovanni would appear and she'd be half-nude. Or half-made-up. She didn't know which would be worse, because the dress demanded maximum work on her face to do it justice.

"I didn't want to tell you over the phone," she said mournfully. "I'd have given anything to tell you to your face but . . . it happened and I've got this ring, this wonderful, dazzling ring, and Marion knows, and maybe other people will notice, because I don't want to take the ring off," she said truthfully, "and the last thing I want is for you to find out before I'd spoken to you. So I'm doing that—telling you."

"But, sweetheart," came her grandpa's worried voice, "who is this man who's captured your heart so quickly? And do you love him? Love him to death?"

She hesitated a fraction of a second and then decided she might as well say what she felt. "Yes!" she wailed. "I'm madly, passionately, confusingly in love! I don't know why, I'm not sure I want to feel like this, but he fills my brain nonstop and I get this great whoosh of emotion whenever I see him and it scares me, because sometimes I think he could ask me to jump off a cliff with him and I'd do it!''

"You must be mad!" said her grandfather, affectionate amusement in his voice. "But who—?" He broke off and she could hear Adriana's excited voice in the background. "What? Yes... Darn it, Tina! Call me later. I gotta go. Lal's out and Adriana's fallen. Bye, thinking of you—*call* me!''

The phone went dead. She stared at it for a moment, still wound up from describing how she truly felt about Giovanni. She'd only done that so her grandfather wouldn't think she was making a rash decision. Hadn't she? But the words had been so easy to say, so very glib and convincing.

Oh, she could *thump* something! She was so stupid! Grandpa thought she was mad. So would others....

Shaking with anger at herself, she felt her body become still, every muscle taut as a tensioned wire. It was her way out! Not madness exactly, but behaving oddly. Tina's rage-darkened eyes glinted. If Giovanni thought he'd feed off her good reputation by being Miss Wonderful's fiancé, then all she had to do was... She grinned broadly. She was the key to his success. Keys could lock—or unlock.

The success of his plans depended on her good reputation, her sane, wise, good-natured self. Therefore, she argued, her eyes dancing in sheer delight, if she acted really strangely and out of character, everyone would think she'd flipped her lid. The dress was a start. Everything she did could be slightly offbeat....

She paused, worrying that in ruining Giovanni's plans she'd ruin the reputation she'd carefully built up as well. Then her furrowed brow cleared. She'd put it all down to stress and keep her fingers crossed that her past record and her good work would make people forgive her anything odd she might do.

With luck, her sudden engagement to Gio would also be seen as one of the crazy stupid things she'd done—and not wise or sensible at all! They might even see him for the manipulating guy he was, using her to get his good name back.

She wouldn't be used! Dammit, he wasn't the only one with grit in his fingernails! No smooth arrogant black-mailer was going to clamber all over *her* to reach his goal!

Her watch flashed alarming figures at her. *Help!* Face. Hair. Dress. Like a whirlwind, she flew into the bedroom, stripping off the robe as she went and emerged twenty minutes later, reeling from the race to be ready and from the startling image of the person she'd changed into.

Scarlet woman. Well, she thought guiltily, wickedly, sneaking yet another astonished glance at herself in the hall mirror, eye-catching it was!

Her hair had been brushed into a gleaming black cap, and then a few wild strands had been teased out. Sexy. With hanks of hair combed forward, her bangs sat lower than usual on her forehead and had the effect of making her startlingly blue eyes, with their carefully applied coats of mascara, look enormous. By using a special foundation, any trace of cute freckles had disappeared, leaving a smooth-all-over glowing tan. She looked all eyes and mouth, she thought breathlessly, dabbing a smear of gloss on her generous scarlet lips, and practiced pouting, laughing at the silly result.

Making a half turn, she checked the lie of the skirt—what there was of it. You couldn't get much material between waist and midthigh. And not much to the top, either, she thought with a giggle, making the giant earrings swing perilously. It was a go-all-out-to-get-him dress—deep scoop neck, tight bodice, flaring rah-rah skirt in layers of taffeta that rustled deliciously as she walked and a back that dipped just below her waist.

And the only way to carry it off, she decided, was to act as brazen as the dress. The doorbell rang. She grabbed her handbag, said a quick prayer of safe deliverance and flew down the stairs, her heart in her throat.

Deep breath. Check—wild bits of hair nicely out of place. She sucked in another breath. Composure. Open door.

"Hi! Are you amazed I'm ready?" she cried smugly, sweeping past Giovanni in quick swaying strides without even looking at him. "Come on, I'm starving!"

Tina looked back over her shoulder brightly, and her control wavered. Partly because he looked absolutely devastating, forcing her heart rate up to ten times above normal. But also because of his infinitely flattering, satisfying response to her appearance.

Even from the dozen or so yards that separated them, she could hear the heavy and labored sound of his breathing, see his chest rising and falling beneath the brilliant whiteness of the tailored jacket. There was a sultriness to his full mouth and a determination about his face that sent small flurries of goose bumps chasing over her skin. He licked his lips, firing such an intensely passionate glance at her that she felt her own lips part of their own accord.

"Something wrong? You said eye-catching." Her voice was husky.

A wry smile tipped one corner of his mouth. "So I did." He still didn't move, but took his time languidly studying her from head to foot in an awestruck caress that flowed over her body like molten fire till she felt she must be the same color as the dress. "Tell your grandfather about your engagement?" he queried casually.

"Yes."

"And?"

"He thinks I'm deranged!"

And perhaps Grandpa was right, she thought, inexplicably feeling as though she were floating on air. Weak, dizzy with excitement and an odd feeling of triumph that he should find her so delectable, she was dimly aware of a faintly savage light in his eyes when he finally crossed to her and wordlessly handed her into the car.

No comment. No compliment or expression of his anger that she'd worn something so totally out of keeping for a demure, decent citizen. But she felt the tension in the car become a tangible, touchable mass of thickened air, heated by the warmth from their two bodies, ignited by the male-female messages passing between them.

"After tonight, you won't wear that dress again," he said in quiet command. "It's not the image I want you to project."

Good. He was annoyed! "You'd prefer little Miss Wonderful in her sensible clothes?" she murmured. "I opted for a bit of allure—"

"Thanks for telling me," he said sarcastically, driving into the restaurant parking lot and sliding the car into a slot beneath a row of flowering dogwood. "I'd already worked that one out. I know about your catty little game."

Quite calmly, he reached out and roughly caressed her knee, pushing up the material in his way in a frantic rustling of taffeta till his fingers were inches from the top of her thigh.

"Gio!" she gasped, her hand wrapping around his wrist. She felt her own warm flesh beneath the tips of her fingers, the resisting steel of his. "Don't! What catty game?" she asked jerkily.

"The game of control," he growled.

In panic, she tried to lift off each finger but the pressure was too fierce. Each one began to crawl inexorably closer to the frilly edge of her red satin briefs. She struggled with the seat belt, trying to wrench her body away, but he hung on grimly.

"I don't know what you mean! Don't be stupid," she said more shakily than she'd planned. "Making me angry won't do you any good! You need me—"

"And you need me," he reminded her with sinister softness.

"Let me go," she pleaded. "For God's sake, Gio!"

"I want you to listen to me," he said tightly. "There are rules in our arrangement, Tina. I'm going to make sure you stick to them. Make sure you know who wears the pants in this relationship. Don't imagine you can use your body to twist me around your little finger. I won't play on that ball field! I am not and never will be the kind of man who'll crawl for a woman's kiss! I'd rather walk away."

"I'm not using my body!" she cried indignantly.

He scowled in sheer exasperation. "You haven't any idea of the difference between truth and lies, have you?" he said in contempt. "At the school earlier, you made it publicly clear that you hadn't thought about me all day, giving the impression that I was doing all the chasing."

"I was busy," she protested.

"People in love think about each other," he said coldly. "You should have let the others think that, even though it isn't true. And now you're putting your all into this dress and making sure I know what your 'all' consists of by having most of it in view so I can get aroused and you can show a whole restaurant full of people that I'm panting for you!"

She glared at him. "It's not for that reason. It's not to entice you. It's for the *role*." The role of a crazed woman, she thought. "I wish I'd worn an old cardigan, jeans and lace-up boots as I originally intended. God, how I hate being bullied and pushed around by you!"

"No more than I disliked being at the mercy of two vindictive bitches ten years ago!" he growled, removing his hand at last. "Now the tables are turned. You jump to my tune. Your life is in my hands and if I want to pull a string and watch you dance, then I will."

"I see," she said. "You want me to swoon at your feet, strew roses in your path—"

"No!" he muttered irritably. "I'd loathe that. I just want you to make like we're in love. That our relationship is one of equality. That you love me as much as I love you and we care deeply for one another. That we wouldn't dream of hurting each other. We must give the impression that we enjoy each other's company and are friends. The relationship is sweet, tender, respectful. Got that?" The darkness in his face was relieved by the two livid spots of color on his high cheekbones.

Tina was silent, lost in her misery. He'd just described her dream, but she was having to act it out. "I hate you! I despise you for what you're doing to me to get what you want!" Her voice broke. "Only a total bastard would treat a woman like this."

"Only a total bitch would deserve it," he grated. "And you've got to learn that in public you must behave like a lady if you want me to behave decently toward you *in private.*"

The threat was clear. It was to show her who was boss. "If you hurt me..." she warned.

"I can think of better ways to show my teeth than by brute force," he said. "I suppose you found it amusing to taunt me with your sexuality in Marion Kent's shop, knowing that you'd be safe because I couldn't respond with her breathing down our necks."

"Wh-wh-what?" she stuttered, dumbfounded.

"You switched yourself on like a damn great neon sign," he said, "advertising the availability of the goods. And you were about to withdraw the offer when it fortunately dawned on me what you were up to. I'm afraid that if you lead me on, you must expect results. Well—" he paused "—you've got results, and some time of my choosing I'll make you finish your performance."

"It wasn't..." Appalled, she realized she couldn't tell him the truth—that she'd been genuinely lost in a world of sensuality in his arms. All she could do was to let him think she'd deliberately given him the come-on. Except that would make her out to be a tease, and she refused to accept that label! "I thought it was right for an engaged woman in...in love," she said huskily.

"Get the hell out!" he snarled. "And put on a smile before you do."

"I can't."

"Then take your time, but find one." He switched on a tape, blasting her with a bouncy pop tune. "Let that soak in and make you feel more lively. Get your expression right. It's important. And remember that there'll be people in there who'll know me, maybe one or two who remember the accident. Be prepared for some hostile glances."

"I know," she said in a low tone. "I'm prepared for that."

"Not yet!" he barked when she sullenly made to open the door. "You don't look anywhere near ready."

"We'll be late for our table," she muttered.

"It'll keep."

"It won't! Lincoln has a cutoff time. I know. My students have worked tables there—"

"He or the maître d' will keep it for me," said Giovanni tightly. "They know who I am. They're aware of the business I'll bring to this town, the people I'll wine and dine. They won't dream of giving me any hassle. That's power, Tina. I have it here in my hand, and now that I've got it I'm not going to let it go."

CHAPTER EIGHT

POWER, she thought tremulously. It made people jump when you snapped your fingers. It changed people. Most times she despised those who used power to manipulate others. But she wished she had some so she could manipulate right now! All she had was her plan to appear as if she was going off the rails, and she'd have to work that plan for all she was worth. The thought of beating him at his own game appealed to her sense of mischief and she smiled.

"Okay, I'm ready," she said cheerfully.

"I've got to hand it to you," he said cynically. "You do know how to switch yourself on."

So did he. They performed beautifully for everyone, holding hands and gazing into each other's eyes when they walked in, not even blinking when there was a gasp of recognition from several parts of the room. Proudly, lovingly, Giovanni escorted her through the crowded restaurant—the inhabitants of Eternity dined early in the way of most Massachusetts people, much to Giovanni's disapproval. His arm supported her and she leaned heavily on him, since her legs were weak with nerves.

Their table was outside on the terrace, with a view of the river. In the balmy evening air, they sat and smiled and stared at each other. The waiter hovered till she and Giovanni finally stopped holding hands and studied the menu. Tina was a little awed by the way he set the pace for the meal and refused to allow the waiter to hurry him.

He ordered champagne with the meal, and when it was poured, he clinked his flute to hers and said quietly, "I'm going to tell you about my background."

Eagerly her eyes flashed up. He'd never spoken about his life before he'd come to Eternity, only saying that it was tough when she'd tried to coax information out of him. "Must you?" she said sweetly.

"You'll need to know when you breathlessly relate every detail about me to your grandfather," he reminded her dryly.

She lowered her eyes and pushed a piece of crab around her plate, feeling a swoop of fear in her stomach as the near future closed in on her. Telling her grandfather the identity of the "love of her life" was going to be as hard as telling Adriana. Making a big effort, she put that from her mind. She had a plan to carry out, a performance to produce. Her knees knocked. Thank heaven Lincoln, the owner of the inn, wasn't there that evening to see. She'd never look him in the eye again.

"If you must. You tell, I'll eat," she said, pretending indifference. "What's this called? It's divine!"

"*Granzeola, moleche e cape sante in saor,*" he supplied lyrically.

"Oh, Gio!" she fluttered, aware of the wine waiter by her arm. "You're the only man who can make crab and scallops in sauce sound sexy! Tell me more about Sicily!" she begged, widening her eyes in awe.

Giovanni seemed to be having trouble keeping control of his mouth. It kept slipping into a grin, instead of staying sultry. Tina laughed and he laughed with her.

"Wicked woman," he said, chuckling. "I don't think either of us have enjoyed ourselves much in recent days. Shall we just have fun this evening?" Disarmed by his open good humor, she smiled and nodded. "Sicilia," he said, his voice flowing with a delicious accent that made her knees tremble.

And love, she thought wistfully. There was deep devotion lurking in that word. When he loved a woman, she'd be cherished like a princess. Hastily she took a gulp of champagne to wash away the lump in her throat—and to give her courage. She'd need it soon.

"Sicily is hard and rugged and beautiful," he said softly.
"The people have a suspicious nature and their lives are
dominated by family honor. Father had a small auto-repair
business in Palermo where we lived, dozens of people, all
packed into one small tenement. A cousin and I shared
shoes. You get very close in a society like that."

A window on his world. The world that had forged
Giovanni and made him deeply suspicious, passionately
suspicious. "I can imagine," she said quietly.

"I doubt it," he said dryly. "It's a different world. Kids
grow up fast in Palermo. I was a skilled mechanic by the
time I was twelve from being at my father's side helping him
every day."

"School?" she queried.

Giovanni speared a piece of duck with his fork and gave
a small rueful laugh. "To be avoided. We had to survive.
That meant everyone had to earn money. I studied late in the
evening after I'd done my stint of lining up with a bucket at
the water pump behind two dozen other kids."

"Tough life," she said in admiration. It had bred a tough
single-minded guy, and now she knew why he'd been so
ambitious to climb the ladder out of the poverty trap.

"It was a good training ground. It meant I wasn't afraid
of the work I had to do when I arrived in the States and discovered to my horror that I had to sit in class with kids
younger than me—or do a sprint and catch up!" He
grinned.

"You were always in the library," she recalled.

"Well there's nowhere to study in a tiny house on the
wrong side of the tracks, is there?" he said quietly. "Without a fierce rage to succeed, it's hard to overcome such dif-
ficulties."

Tina's eyes were riveted to his impassioned face. "I never
knew how hard it was for you. The culture shock must have
been enormous."

He took her hand, kissed the tips of each finger and then
each line of her palm. Tina's heart turned over. "It doesn't
do to let people know how ambitious you are," he said with

a faint smile, nuzzling the soft fleshy pad at the base of her thumb. "You see, it would have scared them. I was hungrier than anyone could ever have believed."

"For wealth?"

"Power. Recognition." He gave her a hard cold stare. "Education."

Feeling uncomfortable, Tina dropped her lashes. "Harvard," she murmured. He'd worked harder than anyone she'd ever known, taking on three jobs so he could buy books and clothes, relieving his parents of that burden.

"It was my dream," he agreed. "When we knew I had a place—and I'd landed scholarships from the Rotary and the Sons of Italy—my parents and I took a trip to Harvard." Slanting a glance at his face, she was mesmerized by its stillness and the sadness of his eyes. "We stopped off to picnic on Boston Common and drove over the Charles River to Cambridge. We strolled around the campus, dreaming—Harvard Square, Winthrop Square, Radcliffe... I was there in my dream. I was mentally walking through those great iron gates on my first day with my future spread in front of me and the security and comfort of my parents financially assured."

"Oh, Gio!" she said huskily, the words catching in her throat.

"Come and dance," he said quietly.

He held her in his arms tenderly, like a lover, as though she were a delicate treasure he'd just acquired. And she rested her uplifted cheek against his and ached for the child who'd lined up at the water pump and grown old before his time, for the desperately ambitious student studying all hours of the night, and now for the man he might have been if he hadn't killed her sister.

Giovanni's breath sighed out gently. "Teenaa."

She quivered, her opposition to him almost demolished by that one sensually spoken word. With gentle fingers, he caught her chin between his thumb and forefinger and turned her head till they were gazing into each other's eyes.

"Mmm?" she said, not trusting her voice.

He let her drown in his black smoldering eyes for a while, and she was so muddled that it seemed to her he looked at her with genuine love.

"I love you," he said softly.

She took a shuddering gasp. Her eyes filled with tears and she was immediately crushed to his shoulder. "Gio! Please!" she mumbled miserably against the suffocating pressure. She felt his mouth nuzzle her ear and wanted to wail.

"Are you crazy?" he growled angrily. "You're supposed to tell me that you love me, too, not look as though I've said I'm leaving you forever!"

Sullenly she forced herself back from him. "I wish you had."

"Say it!" he demanded softly. "Say it!"

"I..." Tina swallowed. "I can't. It won't come out right."

"Then do something. Throw your arms around my neck. Mouth the words so people can see if they're looking— which I imagine they are, because every time you move you make the heart of every man here pump a little faster."

Not yours, though, she thought, her gaze transfixed by the glittering command in his fierce eyes. Her own eyes widened. There was a heavy thud beneath her left breast. Excitement, because she was plastered against his body, she decided.

But she wanted to touch him, to take advantage of the charade. Obediently she wrapped her arms around his neck, caressing the smoothness of the pale soft hair at his nape. He gave a convincing shudder, his breath exhaling audibly, and she threw her head back in ecstasy.

"I love you," she crooned hopelessly. "Oh, Gio, I love you!"

He buried his head against her hair, his hands almost squeezing the breath from her. And as they danced she felt a sweet-sharp torture in her body that made her wonder if she was dreaming or if...if everything he was doing—the tender looks, the love that shone from his eyes, the trembling of his aroused body—was real, and not only did he find her desirable, but a spark of their old relationship was being rekindled, too.

Except that he'd loved Beth, not her. She'd been his escape valve. Beth had denied him sex, which had driven him to seek release for his desperate frustration elsewhere. It was Beth he'd loved and she had to remember that. Giovanni had one thing in his head and one thing only.

Revenge. Two things, she amended. Revenge and sex.

While he murmured seductively in her ear sinfully erotic Italian words that made her wretchedly pliant in his embrace, she reminded herself ruthlessly of his motivations and what drove him. Hunger, a fierce rage to succeed. She must take all those qualities for herself and ruin his chances of being accepted by Adriana and the townspeople—without appearing to do so. Or Giovanni would stay in Eternity forever, and one day she'd be watching him walk into the chapel and come out with a bride on his arm. Which would break her heart.

Just a little while longer in his arms, she told herself guiltily. Swaying dreamily to the music, she abandoned herself to the sinful pleasures—the warmth of his hand on her spine, the gentle pressure that brought their lower bodies into contact, the fire of his loins and the exquisite pain of his murmuring words of love.

"Dessert?" he suggested.

Jerked from her fantasy, she hid her disappointment that the idyll was to finish, leaned back in his strong arms and gave him a flirty glance. "Thought you'd never ask!" she said fervently.

She was shaking with nerves when they sat down because she knew what she was going to do and he didn't. Carefully she studied the menu. "Cream-cheese-and-rum cake sounds gorgeous," she said overbrightly, reaching for her champagne flute. The wine waiter hurried over to lift out the magnum and topped up her glass. "Is that nice?" she asked, handing the dessert menu to Giovanni. While he read, she tipped the whole drink into the floral centerpiece and waggled her glass at the waiter again for a refill.

"Yes, you'd like it…. Don't you think you're going a bit fast on the alcohol, Tina?" He frowned, seeing the topping-up operation in full swing again.

"It never affects me," she said disingenuously, and sipped delicately, eyeing him with huge innocent eyes over the rim of her glass. Inside, she was wishing she didn't have to resort to deceit. She loved him and wanted the world to know. But not him. He'd spend a few weeks making love to her, driving her wild, telling her lies. Then he'd dump her. Never again, she vowed.

"*Tiramisu* and *Fugazza*," ordered Giovanni decisively.

Tina tipped part of a second glass of champagne into the flowers and the rest into the fruit dish, beaming at Gio when he looked up again. "I feel…wunnerful!" she declared.

"You look wonderful." Giovanni reached out for one of the frilly gardenias in the display and lifted it out. The stem seemed alive with bubbles and Tina held her breath, but he merely shook it and carefully dried the stem in his napkin, then leaned over and pushed the flower into her cleavage.

His fingers drifted in a silken caress, and she seemed to be losing her head completely, because she had a terrible urge to wiggle her body at him, lean forward seductively and suggest they go somewhere quiet and private. Her eyes closed to shut the wickedness out. She felt his palm curving around her jaw and the elemental kick of love and need that his brutal gentleness had triggered, and then, to her relief and dismay, the caress, and the exquisite torture, ended.

He sat back, dabbing his mouth with his napkin, his black eyes smoldering and inciting her to all kinds of carnal temptations. "Go easy on the champagne. Perhaps you've had too much." He gestured for the ice bucket to be taken away.

Courage, Tina thought, upbraiding herself. It had to be now, or she'd tell him she didn't care whether he loved her or not. She'd tell him she wanted him—if only for a few weeks.

She had to do it. He had to be embarrassed. People would forgive her, for she was newly engaged and allowed to be a little light-headed from the celebratory champagne. The band had stopped for a break and this was the best time. Screwing up her courage and hoping she had enough credits in her Miss Wonderful bag to afford losing one or two, she sprang up, knocking back her chair and flinging out her arms wildly as if to embrace the whole terrace and restaurant beyond.

"I'm engaged!" she announced exultantly.

"Tina!" muttered Giovanni in a warning tone, while a few people sniggered.

Wrong reaction! Staggering slightly, she dragged the chair back and clambered onto it, winning a few gasps as the taffeta ruffles and a long stretch of leg and thigh came level with everyone's eyes.

"It's a secret, but I can't keep it any longer because I want you all to know how happy I am!" she cried in abandoned glee. "I'm having a resh...reception at the Tamber... Tamblyn housh...House. And you're all invited!" she added, to a mixture of cheers, applause and laughter.

"Come down, sweetheart," said Giovanni fondly, holding up his arms to her.

Every inch the embarrassed, loving fiancé. She grinned. If looks could kill.... "Not finished!" she protested, and placed a reckless foot onto the polished pine table, pushing aside the drunken flowers and fruit with her high-heeled scarlet sandal and stopping for a brief second to admire the way Giovanni caught them and rescued the candles. "There's more," she said in the slow, solemn tones of the very drunk, flashing a triumphant look at the silent Giovanni, who was calmly replacing the fruit in the basket, piece by glistening piece.

"Later, sweetheart," he soothed. Relieved, her nerve failing her, she leaned forward, placing her hands on his broad shoulders, thrilling to the sharp intake of his breath.

The room spun a little. His hands had come to rest around her waist, almost spanning it, and he was lifting her down carefully, placing her gently on her feet and tenderly kissing her nose.

Heaven, she thought, eyes closed, feeling the warm satin lining of his jacket coming around her shoulders. And she snuggled into it, enjoying the sensation of wearing something that was his, sighing softly at the brief impression of... possession and sharing.

"Home," he murmured, a small smile of amusement stabbing her with its sweetness.

"Dessert!" she protested softly.

"Home," he said again, escorting her to the door.

Remembering to sway a little, she gave a little giggle. "The car's over there!" she protested, when he pushed her toward the road.

"We're walking. It'll be good for your head. And I have a rule," he said quietly. "One I've stuck to ever since my uncle was run over by a car right in front of me when I was ten."

Tina shivered inside the jacket, ice crackling down her spine. "Oh! How...how awful!" she said in a wobbly voice, thinking of when he'd had his own accident and had killed Sue and Mike. How terrible for him. She never knew. "What rule?"

"I swore an oath that I would never drive when I'd had a drink or when I was emotionally upset," he replied huskily. "And I never have. Either condition affects judgment."

She remained silent and miserable as they walked because he'd tried to appear noble in her eyes when he was patently lying. He hadn't been drinking that night of Sue's accident, but he'd been highly emotional—and had certainly driven his car.

As they approached her apartment, she began to wonder if he'd say anything about her exhibition in the restaurant. Instead, he thanked her for the evening and said good-night. She stared at him, quite disconcerted, expecting an undignified struggle. After all, he thought she was rather drunk and she *was* wearing a come-hither dress!

"Good night?" she said, blinking uncertainly, then saw the shield of ice form over his eyes.

"Just open the door and put the light on so I know you're safe," he said hoarsely.

"Don't pretend to be gentlemanly and protective now," she said crossly. "No one's looking."

"I know that. Do as I say. Are you going to be all right?"

"Why shouldn't I be?" she asked haughtily, unlocking the door.

"You're drunk, aren't you?" he said dryly.

"Oh! Yes! I'll be okay."

"In that case, good night."

He turned and walked away rapidly, and her brow furrowed. If he'd thought she was drunk, why didn't he make a pass? Puzzling over that, Tina climbed the stairs, half elated with the evening, half anguished by the sweet pain of it, and felt comforted by the fact that his voice had sounded thick with need. Perhaps that was dangerous. But it was undeniably, immensely flattering.

Her apartment was silent and empty. Tina felt suddenly exhausted, and after only a perfunctory wash she crawled into bed. In the morning she ignored the accusing scarlet dress on the floor of her room and set off for work. All day she tried unsuccessfully to put more than half her mind to her job.

The remark Giovanni had made about vowing never to drive after alcohol or when under emotional duress kept coming back to haunt her. Adriana had told her about a Sicilian's vow. It was inviolable. That meant Giovanni was even more dishonorable than she'd ever imagined—*or* that he was telling the truth, which meant he hadn't driven his car on the night of her sister's death. Yet she'd seen him....

Her struggle to work that one out was interrupted by a teacher concerned about Ethan Bertelli's number of detentions. She spent some time tactfully explaining that it might be a good idea to ease up on Ethan, since he had difficulty finding anywhere to study outside of school. Privately she wondered whether to tell Giovanni that a study room at the youth center might be a good idea.

"Tina?"

"What?" The teacher was looking at her in an odd way, and Tina realized she'd been staring into space. "Oh. Sorry. I—"

"Yes, I heard about the engagement," said the teacher with a grin, watching Tina finger the ring she'd been told to wear around her neck on a ribbon. "I think you're a bit crazy. That's my bell for class. Talk tomorrow, huh?"

"Yes. Sure." Delighted that at least one person thought she was crazy, Tina also decided she must be brainless, making arrangements about the youth center. Her intention was to ensure that Giovanni left, having been raked over the coals, before his mother even returned. Yet she couldn't deny that providing better facilities for the deprived students with Gio's help had given her a good feeling.

Her eyes closed in anguish. He'd gotten to her heart too successfully. She wanted him to stay even though she knew Adriana would become disturbed and ill. How selfish could she get?

Wearily she dragged herself through the rest of the day, showing little enthusiasm for what she was doing. And then she had a wonderful idea. Instead of going to Ipswich to shop, she spent some time cleaning up the old motorcycle that had been in the back of the garage ever since she'd abandoned it for the first car her grandfather had done up for her. It didn't look too bad. Rather racy in fact! Most people would have forgotten the brief six months she'd ridden around on it and they'd be surprised to see her wearing leathers—if they still fit. She grinned. And they did—just.

Feeling delighted with her vastly different image, she drove around town looking for Giovanni. She eventually spotted him charming some unsuspecting child, and she drew up at the curb with an impressive roar just as the beaming Giovanni bid the guy farewell and turned to cross the road.

He gave a double take and frowned. Slowly she undid the strap under her chin and removed the helmet, shaking out her hair.

"It's me!" she said unnecessarily, and giggled at his lack of speech. But that wasn't surprising. Instead of a conventional car, she was sitting astride a gleaming motorbike! "Tina. Remember? We got engaged—"

"And you got drunk in front of half of Eternity. Yes, I remember," he said dryly, recovering himself with impressive speed. "Is this yours?"

"Yes. I've had it for years."

"I remember," he said gravely. "Distinctly." And his eyes told her that what he remembered most was the fun they'd had when they'd used it for a change on some of their dates.

Her smile wavered. Frantically she pumped up her smile again and said, "Isn't the bike wonderful?"

"Wonderful. It must be virtually a classic now. Love the leathers."

"Bit hot now that I've stopped." She frowned, stripping off the jacket to reveal a skinny vest. His reaction was spoiling the fun. He was supposed to be horrified. "You don't think it'll spoil my image, do you?" she asked with wide-eyed innocence.

"It'll be a reckless road that tangles with you, let alone anyone human. And your students will be your slave," he replied. "You do look hot, though. I have an idea," he said, his eyes alight with fun. "Take me for a ride, then we'll pick up your bathing suit and a change of clothes and you can come to my house for a swim and supper. You need to familiarize yourself with the layout and where we're holding the reception, so you can sound knowledgeable."

It was too appealing an offer to turn down. Swimming would be blissful, and so would walking in the gardens. "Okay," she said, glad of a chance to show off the bike— and herself. All she needed was to build up a reputation as a kook!

Riding around town with Giovanni plastered to her back was an experience she didn't want to repeat, however. Especially as her plan to shock people didn't work at all. To her eternal chagrin, everyone seemed glad she'd shed her goody-two-shoes image and was striking out. The consensus was that Giovanni was doing her a lot of good, that she'd been too staid and serious, taking little enjoyment out of life—and he was taking her "out of herself"!

She couldn't believe it. Giovanni looked more and more smug, and he asked advice about wedding plans from any likely woman they met. Simmering beneath her shaky smile, Tina suffered earnest conversations about flower girls and musicians, jokes about getting a limo on the cheap and advice to Giovanni to put a hold on those lawn sprinklers so the high heels of female guests wouldn't sink into mud.

The students were no better. Gloomily Tina pressed down on the kick starter after Josh Davis and his friends had waved her down and spent half an hour rhapsodizing over the bike and saying how "cool" she was. Far from doing her image damage, her behavior was enhancing it!

"Well, that went off successfully," said Giovanni in satisfaction as they climbed off the bike in front of her place. "That was a great idea of yours to go high profile. Well done."

"Christine Bertrand is arranging for her husband, Paul, to do an article in the paper!" she wailed. "It'll be all over town. You're giving me no time to prepare your mother. I can't cope! You're a ruthless brute!"

"Must see the florist," he murmured. "Who *are* you going to have as your flower girl?" Her scowl only made him laugh. "If you knew how gorgeous you look, with your hands on your hips, those ridiculous leathers molding your body...."

Her quick glance down made her smile wryly. He was laughing and his laughter was so infectious she found the corners of her mouth lifting, too. "Rehearsal dinner!" she said, mimicking his earnest tones of half an hour ago. "And 'What's your opinion of fingerless mitts,' indeed! As for that deep discussion about our linen trousseau...! Words fail me!"

"Almost failed me once or twice," he said huskily. "Thinking of you, stretched out on my satin sheets."

"I won't be," she reminded him tartly, then raced indoors to get her bathing suit and a change of clothes while he went to retrieve his car.

When they arrived at his house, he turned to her with a grin. "Gets a bit difficult to work out what's real and what isn't sometimes, doesn't it?"

"Only for you. So, where's this pool?" she asked ungraciously.

"You're wonderful!" Giovanni said laughing. "Do you know that everyone in town is gossiping and saying how romantic it is, you and me, getting together after all these years? Love triumphing despite everything that's happened—like Romeo and Juliet, someone said."

"Nauseating," she said airily.

"There are various things you need," he said in amusement, "but the first is a swim, as I promised. Come this way."

He led her around the huge clapboard-fronted house and by the conservatory, full of tropical plants. Tina paused there, inhaling the rich perfumes. Adriana would love it, she thought, and hurriedly moved on, walking beneath the carefully clipped arch of an old yew hedge.

"It's breathtaking!" she declared. "I'd forgotten how lovely it was."

The lawn stretched away from the house like a matt green carpet, with colorful herbaceous borders on each side backed by ornamental shrubs and trees.

Giovanni pointed out a stand of enormous rhododendrons. "They originated in the Himalayas. The realtor said that Azariah's wife was Emmelina Fox, a friend of a Victorian man—Wilson, I think—who went plant hunting. He provided specimens for Kew Gardens in London and the Arnold Arboretum in Boston, and filled the Fox gardens in Cornwall with exotic plants."

"I have a connection with this house, too," she said wryly. "My ancestor, Tiernan Murphy, worked for the Tamblyns."

"Did he? I have something else in mind for *you* while you're here," he said, his voice dropping to a provocative pitch.

"We are pretending affection. We are simulating sexual compatibility," she reminded him quickly. "Any sweet glances you get from me are feigned. In reality, my response to you is as energetic as those marble statues in those niches."

"Uh-huh."

She glared at the sardonic agreement and followed him to the orchard, where the young fruit promised a bumper crop. Beyond were sunlit meadows and paddocks where purebred horses grazed. "Yours?" she asked.

"Mine." Her face fell. Giovanni had well and truly moved in. "This way," he murmured, sounding amused. "You can change in the room off the orangery. You'll see the pool from there. I'll join you in a moment."

They swam and lazed in the sunshine, clutching iced soft drinks brought to them by a friendly Sicilian, and because the day was so idyllic and the sun warm and drugging, Tina relaxed and began to chat easily with him as she always used to.

With interest, she stared up at the mansion with its dark green shutters, delicate slender chimneys and widow's walk on the top, where Azariah's wife must have paced, waiting for him to return from his long sea voyages. Had she loved her husband? Tina wondered. Did she know the pain of loving a man she couldn't trust?

"Do you remember how we envied Beth for living here?" he said, breaking in on her thoughts.

Tina smiled wanly. He didn't have to rub it in. He was now wealthier than Beth and her parents. "There wasn't any love in the house," she said stiffly. "She preferred our place with its chaos and affection."

"I intend to fill this house with love," he said softly, running his fingers up her arm. When she jerked away, appalled at what he'd said, he transferred his interest to her thigh, and she felt her body shudder in desire before she jumped up irritably. He impaled her with his glittering black gaze. "We all spend our lives searching for the place where we can be happy," he continued. "Where we can feel at home and put down roots, where we can stretch our lives beyond the merely mechanical. I've always known where my home would be. Here. With an adoring wife, friends, family, children."

"Children!" she gasped wretchedly.

"I will have my share one day, God willing."

The pain cut through her, slicing her body as surely as if someone had taken a meat cleaver to it. And she was left weak and shaking with the awful inevitability of his future and hers.

"I think I'll go now," she said, choking out the words.

Giovanni rose and tipped up her chin, so that she was unable to stop him from seeing the tears in her eyes. Inexplicably he kissed her eyelids and she groaned, sobbing wildly for the love she could never express.

Gently his mouth sipped the tears now cascading down her face. And dumb with misery, she let him kiss her on the mouth, her hand straying to his sun-warmed cheek and stroking it with tender love as if it were her own child's face.

A torrent of wonderful, liquid Italian words tumbled from his mouth as he gazed at her, drowsy with desire, massaging the back of her neck with a delicacy that had her crying out in small gasps of pleasure.

"Tina . . ." he growled thickly.

She was in his strong arms, her almost naked body pressed to his bare chest, and they were moving. Giovanni was taking her into the house. Churning emotions kept her silent. Her enormous frightened eyes saw elaborate brocade curtains, an ornate plaster ceiling, a crystal chandelier. She tried to speak, but he kissed her, stopping to do so for a brief fierce moment that took her breath away. She knew she had to start finding her voice, her senses, her desire to fight, all over again because the touch of his mouth on hers, the promise of his body giving her what she desired, was becoming too tempting.

A vast ceiling. A hallway. The suspended mahogany staircase. Paintings, flowers, draperies, antiques, a canopied bed....

A canopied bed!

"Gio! No!" she breathed, beginning to struggle, lurching half-out of his arms. Her hands were shaking, trembling against his bare chest. And against her fluttering fingers his heart beat like a great steam engine. She shot him an astonished look and was lowered onto the bed. Then his body covered hers, the cool antique quilt beneath her, his warm, infinitely touchable flesh above.

His long lashes swept down as he surveyed her taut breasts straining against the thin material of her suit, and when he raised his eyes again she saw that they were glowing with black fire, forcing life and energy and a wild ecstatic joy into her. She drew a deep breath as her emotions gathered strength and clamored for release.

"You are beautiful, Tina!" he said softly. "And far too wanton for any normal man."

His fingers stroked her bare shoulders, swept away the straps with dismissive contempt. And her pulse thundering in her ears, she anticipated the touch of his mouth on her naked breasts with deliciously sharp stabs of desire that made her whimper softly in her constricted throat.

"Sweet and gentle," he muttered, as if to himself. A harsh agonized groan trembled on his lips, and then she felt the light brush of a finger across the thickening dark peaks of her breasts. "Do you want me?"

Lightly, his mouth sipped each quivering tip. He lifted his head a little and emphasized his question with an arching brow when she made no answer.

"Do you want me?" he asked again, softly surrounding one hard nipple with his lips. Tina gritted her teeth against the desire to say yes—but she groaned aloud because his mouth had begun to tug, to suckle, and she couldn't, wouldn't hold down the flames licking through her and consuming her very being.

"Yes!" she whispered, aghast at her weakness.

Her body lifted to him. He kissed her long and hard and slow like a drowning man taking a drink.

And then his velvet warmth was gone. Slowly she opened her eyes. He stood by the window, staring out at the garden. Bewildered, her eyes dark with shame and humiliation, Tina saw him turn, and she cringed back in alarm at the coldness written in every line of his face.

"I told you that your behavior in the jewelry shop deserved a proper response," he said.

She gave a small cry of denial, but she knew with a sinking heart that he had been punishing her. Nothing more. He'd wanted her; that had been impossible to hide, and he still was ferociously aroused. But revenge came even before his own pleasure. Her body chilled. He'd deny himself sexual gratification to satisfy his need for vengeance. God, he was merciless!

Without a word, she drew up her straps, rolled off the bed and wrapped the quilt around her trembling body. He sprang to the door and barred the way. "Let me out of here!" she demanded.

"Sure," he said tightly. "First, you get your behavior into line. You will not jeopardize my ambitions. I know what you've been doing—do you think I'm stupid? I'm tuned in to you, Tina. I know how your mind works and what you're thinking. I can outwit, outfight and outseduce you anytime! You will not go back on your word. Promise me now you'll put everything you've got into making this temporary engagement work or, by God, I swear I'll strip you naked and ravish you with such devastating effect you will never be able to look at another man again!"

His arm snaked out, roughly dragging her toward him, and her legs buckled in fear. On her knees, she clung to his legs for a moment, loathing him, frightened out of her wits. And he was suddenly on the floor with her, kissing her brutally, forcing her mouth to open. The intimate kisses branded her as his possession. His hands, ruthlessly drawing away the quilt and making her body writhe in involuntary delight, ripping her suit—

"Oh!" she gasped in horror, her eyes limpid and fixed on his. She twisted in terror, but her body was slow and the movement became a voluptuous invitation.

"You want me!" he growled.

"No!" she denied angrily.

But there was a warmth at the top of her thighs, and Giovanni's touch had stilled her to a tense, fierce yielding. Her whole body melted willingly in his hands, and his roaming mouth and the sweetness of his cruelly gentle caresses washed a deep love through her that no barrier could hold back.

"I want you," he said roughly. "I want you, and I will have you. I could walk away, even now—"

She jammed her lips together, knowing she'd been about to beg him to stay.

His eyes mocked her. "I choose not to this time," he said savagely. "So I will kiss you on your heart... and on your lips... feel the silk of your beautiful sensual body... taste your flesh...."

Tina groaned and jerked spasmodically. With a graceful movement, he drew her to her feet where she swayed, dizzy and supine, in his arms.

"Dance with me," he murmured.

"D-dance?" she whispered with a quiver of excitement.

"Dance."

The movement of his body was driving her wild. He held her eyes with his and she stared into the smoldering blackness like an addict, unable to get enough of him, unable to press herself close enough, to kiss enough, to touch. Their hands explored, their mouths devoured, and she felt the rising urgency within her, the fluidity of her body as their dance became more intimate, more tantalizingly tormenting.

Tina was angry. He was denying her, deliberately denying her! With a hard tug of her hand, she brought his mouth down to hers and kissed him till she was breathless. "I hate you, I hate you! Make love to me!" she demanded in confusion. "Damn you, Giovanni! Please!"

His face became gentle and loving. "With pleasure," he said. "With enormous pleasure."

The breath in her body flowed out and she closed her eyes. This once. Only this once, she promised herself helplessly as he carried her to the bed.

CHAPTER NINE

ONCE, TWICE, THREE times. Each more tender, more passionate and more loving than before, till she thought her heart would burst with the wonder of it all. Her head, too, was spinning with unspoken emotion. Giovanni paused above her, his eyes glittering and unfathomable, while she cried in anger that he should withhold her pleasure and break the delirious excitement even for one second.

"Say you love me!" he demanded hoarsely.

"It's sex," she whispered. "Only sex. You're right, I am nothing better than a wanton—"

Silken heat burned within her. "Say you love me," he growled ruthlessly.

Tina closed her eyes, moving her body sinuously, but Giovanni clenched his jaw and scalded her with his eyes, refusing her mute plea and tormenting her with the flicker of his tongue on each trembling breast. "I love you," she said helplessly. "I love you."

IT WAS LATE, the moon shining in on their naked bodies, turning him to a silver god for her to worship. "I have to go," she mumbled weakly, wishing she could stay and sleep the night in his arms. Her body lay cupped in his and was content. She felt a deep satisfaction in her whole being, as if their lovemaking had swept away all the intervening years of sexual emptiness and her agonizing over his shattered life.

His profile was dear to her eyes, and she longed to stroke it with her finger. He turned and smiled at her and it was so sweet, so tender, that she sighed. Inside, she said *I love you* over and over again like a glorious and secret litany while he

ran his hand over her body and she steeled herself to the inevitable knowledge that he was using her as he'd used her
before—to ease his sexual hunger.

Whereas she had a hunger of the soul.

"Let me dress you."

"I can do it!" she said savagely.

"No, you can't. You're exhausted."

Cross because that was true, she languidly strolled to the
bathroom to shower while he watched her from the bed, and
when she reached the privacy of the cool mint green room
and its huge display of freesias, she collapsed to the floor in
a despairing heap, surrounded by the sweet perfume.

What had she done? Her horror-struck eyes lifted to the
reflection in the floor-length mahogany mirror, taking in the
ripe womanly body, lush and glowing from Giovanni's in-
toxicating caresses. She closed her eyes and could still feel
his lingering mouth and hear his soft cry as the world exploded around them. Wearily she crawled to the shower and
hauled herself upright, brutally punishing herself with ice
water.

He dried her with a warm fluffy towel—silent, thorough
and gentle—but wouldn't meet her eyes. He dressed her because she couldn't lift a tired hand and because it was wonderful to feel his cool touch—for the last time, she vowed
fiercely, lashing herself with scorn and bitter censure.

"I'll drive you home."

Briefly acknowledging that with a lift of her heavy head,
she saw his expression with some shock. Venomous.

Bewildered, she tried to understand why, but her brain
had gone the same way as her common sense and wasn't
around anymore. They said no more to each other as he
drove, and she staggered out of the car on his arm, upset by
the way he flinched when she leaned closer momentarily for
greater support.

His hand was on the key, when the door suddenly opened
and she fell into the arms of her astonished grandfather.

"Adriana!" she gasped.

"She's not here. What the...? Tina, that's...!"

Squashed against her grandfather's big brawny chest, Tina felt his shock of recognition and blushed in horror that she was fresh from her lover's bed. "Yes. It's Gio," she said miserably. "I'm engaged to Gio. I love him." She looked into her beloved grandfather's face, a desperate plea on her face. "I love him, Grandpa!"

Dan Murphy's blue eyes narrowed shrewdly. "Come in," he said grimly.

Giovanni looked him straight in the eye and frowned. "She's tired!" he protested with a protective firmness.

Dan glared, a grudging admiration in his expression. "Then you can do the talking."

"Very well, sir, I will," replied Giovanni, showing his habitual courtesy to his elders.

"Why are you back?" asked Tina shakily, pressing a hand to her aching forehead. "Adriana..."

"She's safe in Rockport with Lal. I was worried about you. I came to see how you were and I've been waiting for hours."

"I'm sorry you've been alone," said Giovanni, as if expecting to hear otherwise.

"Not at all. I've been busy selling the garage," retorted her grandfather, grinning with delight.

"Oh, Grandpa!" she cried, suddenly elated. Her eyes shone deep sea blue in her white face. This was her release! Giovanni could no longer blackmail her. They could go away for a while, hide, keep Adriana from him.... Her mind whirled with possibilities. "Tell me," she demanded urgently. "Who? What's to happen? Is it certain? What about the part-timers? Will they have jobs?"

"There you go, thinking of everyone but yourself!" grumbled her grandfather, settling her firmly on a comfortable armchair in the sitting room. She passed a hand over her forehead, tired, bewildered and trembling.

"Are you all right, Tina?" asked Giovanni with concern.

Her eyes flew to his. Several long seconds passed. "Yes," she said, dropping her gaze. Perhaps this would be the last time she saw him. Her tears fell silently.

"Don't cry, sweetheart." Her grandfather had been studying her carefully, but now he smiled and patted her knee. "Everything's working out fine. The part-timers will be kept on, and I have signed, sealed and delivered a contract that not even Houdini could wriggle out of. And what a price! We're rich. We can find a house with a garden." His glance lifted to Giovanni. "You won't cause trouble with your mother now, will you? She won't see you and that's that."

"I know," Gio said quietly.

Tina felt the worrying change in his tone and brushed the back of her hand across her eyes. Giovanni leaned forward, handing her a clean white handkerchief, and she wiped her tears away, worrying at the brittle line to his mouth. She overcame the urge to run to him. Instead, she tipped up her chin bravely. She was free of him forever.

"It's . . . great news!" she said, trying to feel enthusiastic. All their dreams had just come true, so why wasn't she singing for joy? "Who . . . who's the buyer?"

Her grandfather searched his mind. "An agent, acting for some multinational developer. . . ."

"For me," said Giovanni quietly. "I'm the developer."

Tina's head whipped around, her eyes accusing. "You?"

"I arranged for my agent to make a bid. The garage is mine," he said coldly. Her haunted eyes grew larger and larger.

Dan Murphy gave a muttered exclamation. "Giovanni! What the devil . . . !"

"I'll explain, sir. Tina, you look terrible. Go to bed. I want to talk to your grandfather about the arrangements, and I imagine he has a few things to say to me."

"So have I!" she snapped, her eyes blazing, her body trembling with rage. And questions. She had a dozen. Like why he'd bought the garage when it meant losing one of his means of blackmail. "Why have you done this?" she demanded fiercely.

"Darling," he said, the warning plain in his eyes, "we're engaged." *Remember that,* his expression said. "I am a businessman and I look after family. It was the obvious move. Your grandfather wanted to sell. I made that possible for him." He smiled. "That's what I like to do—make people happy."

"You did it to buy Grandpa's goodwill!" she accused, shaking with anger and exhaustion.

"Please, Tina," said her grandfather, suddenly looking rather old and frail. "I think it would be better if Giovanni and I had our talk. He's right. You look tired and pale, and you've got a long day at school tomorrow. I'm old enough and wise enough to pull a few punches and throw a couple of my own if necessary. Go to bed, sweetheart."

Mutinously she glared at the two men, but it was a very feeble mutiny. Normally she would have battled to get her own way. Tonight she was too tired to argue. "I want a brief word with Giovanni first," she said stiffly, and walked into the hall. When he followed her, she said coldly, "Don't imagine that what happened between us was anything other than a mistake." Her icy eyes burned into his. "I despise you, Giovanni!" she said scornfully, hating herself for giving in to him, hating him again—again!—for seducing her. "I'll go through with this farce if I have to. But any chance I get, I'll slide out of it! And you can be sure that the moment I don't have to suffer your disgusting mauling and crude animal lust, I'll be free to dance and sing and find some joy in my life again, because you've sure ripped any happiness I ever felt out of my existence!"

Proud, amazed at her control, she walked away from the impassive Giovanni and tumbled wearily into bed.

STIRRING her coffee the next morning, she listened to her grandfather's congratulations with openmouthed astonishment. "You're *pleased* we're engaged?"

"I am. He's a good man, Tina Murphy. The past is done and finished with. He's been punished enough." Her grandfather frowned. "Perhaps too much. I want to show everyone in Eternity I'm behind him one hundred percent, so I'm doing a bit of part-time work with him."

"*What?*" she wailed, feeling betrayed. "Why?"

"I told you," said her grandfather. "It's my dream—"

"Oh, he's into dreams in a big way," she said bitterly.

"That's not like you!" chided her grandfather gently. "I'll forgive you since you're under stress. He intends to turn the whole site—here and the Alden place—into one beautifully designed auto shop, with a showroom of the most elegant classic cars you've ever seen in your life. Rolls-Royces, Bentleys—"

"I've heard the list," she said sourly, scowling at the enthusiastic way he was buttering his toast. Gio had bought her grandfather and all the goodwill that came with Dan Murphy. A subtle move, one offering her grandfather everything he wanted. God, he was clever!

"You know I've always longed to work on classic cars," her grandfather said with a faraway look in his eyes. "The weddings will be even more special for the happy couples. They'll get to sweep to and from the chapel in sublime luxury! Can't you see how great it'll be for the town?"

"Yes," she said dully, pushing her food grumpily around the plate. "I can."

"The Alden place will be demolished—how he persuaded them to sell, I don't know—and it'll no longer be a danger or an eyesore. That's good," he said approvingly. "Folks from Boston and the whole of Sussex County will be attracted to the idea of using a Bentley or an old Bugatti for their wedding day. They're beautiful machines, Tina!" he enthused. "We can employ more people, more students on work-placement programs...."

"That'll be nice," she mumbled. She was getting the impression that Giovanni had his feet so firmly under the table in this town that he'd never go. And where did that leave her?

"I'm heading for some enjoyment in my old age," Dan went on. "Gio's a great guy. You're lucky you both have gotten over the past and not let it stand in your way."

"I give up!" She heaved a tremendous sigh. Gio had totally won her grandpa over. It was unbelievable. "What about his mother?" she asked anxiously. "Don't you know what this'll do to her? If she hears a whisper of his name, she'll be in need of medical treatment!"

Dan fixed his granddaughter with a stern eye. "I told Adriana after you phoned that you'd fallen in love. She's thrilled. She only wants the best for you, Tina—she loves you so much. You'll do your best to coax her round, because that's the right and Christian thing to do. You have a way with her and know how far to go. You could do it if you tried. I think you should."

"Oh, Grandpa!" she said helplessly, knowing he was right. "If... if it doesn't work?"

"We'll cross that bridge when we come to it. At worst, we'd have to accept that and keep her away from this end of town and split our lives into two when you get married."

"Married!" she breathed.

Her grandfather smiled warmly. "I know how much you two loved one another when you were younger. It was beautiful to see. You had eyes for no one else. What happened was terrible, a dreadful visitation on the two of you, but... I've never said this to a living soul, but I've wondered sometimes if Giovanni was speaking the truth when he said Beth was driving. He worked with me. We sweated on difficult jobs together. You get to know people under hard conditions, and I never knew a more honest, more decent human being."

Tina lifted reproachful eyes to his. Even her own grandfather was set to betray her. "The weight of evidence—"

"I know, I know." He sighed. "Funny, though, I've been talking to Adriana this holiday about family and children, hoping to jolt her mind. I think she's beginning to remember a few things about Gio. You've got to promise to give it your best shot. I'll do my bit, too. That's all we can do. She wants to meet your 'beau.' She might remember you're engaged when she comes home, but if not, we must jog her memory and start talking about weddings. Then you tell her Gio is back and see what happens."

Tina pushed her pineapple muffin away, feeling sick at the thought. Perhaps he was right—to a point. She would refuse to destroy Adriana's delicate state of health for Giovanni's sake, however much everyone thought of him. "Okay, I'll try," she said reluctantly. "I'll do my best, Grandpa. I'm not pushing her, mind!" she added with a dark frown.

"You'll do it because you're a good girl. Oh, I'll give you a wedding like you've never seen!" he said fondly. "You and Gio will exchange your vows in the chapel and you'll stay together for the rest of your lives. I know that's true already, because you two look at each other with such love it makes me choke up. God bless you both!"

"I—I have to go to work," she said, her voice husky with misery. And she jumped up from her chair and hurried into her bedroom.

Why was everyone blinded by Giovanni's charm? How could even the sanest and wisest person see no further than the easy smile, the sugarcoated words? He flattered people. He gave them what they most wanted to hear and they thought he was a great guy in return. Wretched man! He could manipulate steel girders with that smile if he tried!

In a tearing rage, she thundered down the stairs yelling goodbye to her grandfather, hurled open the door and came to a skidding halt. Giovanni was outside, cool and glacial in a honey beige linen suit that had been poured over his beautiful body. She allowed herself one heart-stopping look and stormed over to her motorbike.

"I'm taking you to work," he said firmly, catching her up and whirling her around. "That's what lovers do. They can't bear to be away from one another for longer than they have to."

"I'm not going directly to work—I'm going to see Jim Falconer," she snapped, her eyes daring him to stop her. "He's one of the guys you threw out of school, a pain in the neck like you. It must be catching because he's the one who lives in your old house."

A dark brow winged up. "I remember. I'll take you there. I'm your loving boyfriend, remember?"

"I won't get far with Jim if you're around," she declared. "I'm trying to help him...." She hesitated. Maybe Giovanni could offer him a job. If he saw his old home and heard how hard it was for Jim to cope with his grandmother, maybe a spark of compassion would cause Gio to be generous for once. "All right," she said casually. "I give in."

They made the short drive, then pointing to the building some yards from his old house, Gio said, "I'll park beside that disused factory."

"Fine," she said. "Now I've got to persuade him to leave Ethan alone, among other things."

"Optimist. Best of luck." Giovanni moved the car to the parking spot, leaned back in the seat and turned on the stereo.

When she emerged from Jim's a while later after a depressingly unsatisfactory chat, she couldn't see the car for a moment. Giovanni had reversed the car right under an oak tree.

"How did it go?" he asked quietly.

"Not great." She sighed. "I'm at my wit's end. Ethan has the brains to do well. His secret ambition is to be a doctor, but Jim..." She shrugged. "Can we sit here a moment?" she asked wearily. "I need breathing space before tackling the problems on my desk."

Gloomily she studied the street. The old Kowalski house, where Jim now lived, was the only clapboard house not in dire need of repair. Giovanni's parents had kept it in good condition and it had remained so. Her eyes flickered over to him. He was looking at the house as though it held ghosts.

"Is this difficult for you?" she asked.

"It's a time long gone. A life so different from the one I lead today I can hardly believe it happened," he said quietly. "That's the grandmother, isn't it?"

She turned her head to look. "Yes—and Jim, with a broom!" To her surprise, Jim hugged his grandmother, lifting her off her feet in a teasing, affectionate way and, tugging his forelock in mock deference, began to sweep the porch.

Tucked away in the shadows, Tina and Gio were able to watch unobserved while Jim did various chores. As he clipped the hedge his grandmother sat in her rocking chair on the porch and chatted animatedly with him. Sometimes Jim laughed, sometimes his grandmother did. All in all, thought Tina, it was a scene of domestic bliss. Jim Falconer did have another side. Giovanni's sharing in her discovery was a bonus.

"I'd like to find Jim a job," she said quietly. "In fact, I'd like to find work for Glen and Ethan, too. Gio...I'd like them to work with Grandpa at the garage—"

"Out of the question."

She turned eagerly to plead her case. "It could be the making of them! Ethan desperately needs the experience for his grades. He's in a technical course and has been doing badly at school. Grandpa can make a silk purse out of a sow's ear and—"

"No."

"You will be offering work placements at the garage, won't you?" she asked cautiously. "Grandpa always—"

"No. I'm canceling them."

"You can't! It's become usual practice!" she cried in horror. "The students and staff rely on the placements, and they've become a key part in some of the grades! Is this some kind of spiteful revenge?"

"No." Giovanni turned his icy black eyes on her. "I don't want to get involved in work placements or with anyone you're dealing with. I don't want us to have any contact at all in the future. If the garage takes students, that will mean collaborating with you, and frankly I would rather shut the whole place down."

"I can't believe this!" she gasped. "I have guys with Grandpa who had particular difficulty finding places! They're all crazy about cars, and student car mechanics mean huge savings! Grandpa's brilliant with—"

"No!" he snapped. "Don't you hear what I'm saying? I want nothing to do with you!"

She stared at him, appalled, the whole of her program—and the needs of her students—suddenly jeopardized. "As a favor, then," she said tremulously. "As a favor to me!"

"I owe you no favors!" he growled angrily.

Tina flinched. "But...car jockeys. For the weddings. Surely that would be okay...."

"Only if they apply to me directly," he said coldly. "I'm bringing in my cousins to staff the garage complex. I won't need students or ex-students."

She flushed. "There'll be a lot of opposition to that. Bad feeling—"

"Nothing I can't handle. I won't put strangers above family."

"That won't do much for your rehabilitation," she said waspishly.

"The question won't arise till I've built the complex, and by then I'll have established my reputation," he drawled.

"You'd get a lot of instant admiration if you took on Jim and Glen *now,*" she said slyly. "They could do with the money. Aren't you prepared to give them a helping hand to lift themselves out of the poverty trap?"

He looked at her in grudging amusement. "You know where to hit a guy's conscience, don't you? Unfortunately you're right. It would be in my interests. Okay—providing your grandfather liaises with you, and I have nothing to do with them. You can tell them I'll give them a trial run."

"And Ethan, for his grade?"

"Don't push your luck!" he said irritably. "I don't want you to be involved in the garage. I particularly don't want anything to do with you other than what's strictly necessary. Is that clear?''

"Yes," she muttered. Then her head snapped up with pride. He wasn't interested in her now that he'd had what he wanted from her—sex. She'd given in to him with unseemly eagerness again. A deep, souring resentment, a horrifying mortification washed through her in sickening waves. "Nor do I want to be involved longer than I have to with a coldhearted Casanova!" she accused.

"That describes me perfectly," he growled, his eyes glittering dangerously. "And you'd better remember that!"

With a harsh cry, she slumped back in the soft leather seat. For several moments Giovanni sat there, his shoulders heaving while he glowered at Jim and the evidently warm and affectionate relationship he had with his grandmother. The scene didn't seem to relieve Giovanni's temper, and she wondered if he was thinking of his mother.

"I'll be late," she mumbled hoarsely, wanting to get away from him and the pain he brought her.

"I don't drive unless I'm calm."

Tina heaved an exasperated sigh and waited, worried about the future, worried sick about her promise to tell Adriana that Gio was back. Worried to screaming point about life after Gio....

Work that day was impossible, but everyone made allowances for her, smiling fondly and confiding to her that word had gotten out, and even her secretary seemed genuinely delighted. *I hate him, I loathe him,* Tina kept muttering to herself, and spent more time spearing bits of paper on her "pending" spikes than was absolutely necessary because she was releasing some of her anger—mentally substituting Giovanni's heart for the inoffensive scraps of paper.

The whole week was painful. All her waking time away from work seemed to be spent with Giovanni. Meals with him and her grandpa were excruciating, because the two men got on so well and she spent half the time hating Giovanni and half of it desiring him. No wonder the pounds were dropping off her!

"I've got something to show you," Gio said coldly one day at lunchtime when she slid into the familiar comfort of his car.

"Not the wedding cake, I hope!" she said, knowing he'd threatened to make her choose one. "And I *refuse* to try on any more wedding dresses. It makes me sick—"

"A crashed car."

"What?" she gasped. "Gio, if you're trying to hurt me..."

"You?" He turned onto the lighthouse road, his expression remote and his mouth pinched with tension. "Have you any idea what it does to me every time I see an automobile accident? And this time, it's particularly painful!"

"I'm getting out," she muttered, wrestling with the door handle.

"That'll do Jim a lot of good," he grunted.

"Jim?"

"He took a little joyride," Giovanni said tightly. "In one of my newly imported Bentleys. That's what's left of it." He pointed.

Tina stared in horror. The beautiful silver-gray car had been driven through a low sea wall and was hanging over the five-foot drop to the beach, its front end crumpled beyond repair. "Jim?" she asked, white faced.

"Ran off," he said heavily. "Someone saw him. He wasn't hurt—jumped out before it hit the wall, thank God. But I could murder him!" He glowered. "I gave him a chance and look what he did with it! The waste! The sheer, unadulterated waste!"

"I'm sorry about the car..." she began.

He turned to her angrily. "Car? I don't give a damn about the car! It's... I trusted him! I talked to him and his grandmother, told him about myself, how I'd made the big time. I convinced him that everyone had a chance in life. I gave him hope. He let me down."

"And me," she said unhappily, staggered that Giovanni had tried so hard with Jim. Perhaps he saw himself, ten years ago, she mused.

"No more chances. No more lame ducks, Tina. No students."

"A second chance, please..."

"I don't give second chances."

"It's what you're demanding from all of us!" she pointed out. "And we're giving you one, aren't we? And if you put an exclusion zone around the garage as far as students are concerned, there'll be bad feelings."

"Then I'll close the damn garage *now* and the wedding business can go hang!"

"The whole town's involved!" she protested. "There are half a dozen weddings I know of this weekend. Eternity needs the cars. They'll never get anyone else at this short notice."

"Then you get word around and make it clear I've been let down. You're upset about that. You support me in my desire to stick with family only."

"I—I can't do that."

"You'd better, Tina," he snarled. "Or I'll ruin the wedding arrangements. Do you want to upset the happy brides and make their special day a misery?"

"I loathe you!" she spat.

"I will get my way," he said in a soft growl. "In everything. His hand jerked her toward him and he crushed his mouth on hers in a brief brutal kiss. "I don't care how I get it," he said, gazing at her angry face. "Only that I do. Support my decision. I use members of my family because I can trust them. You understand this. You feel disappointed, but see that I have no alternative. Yes?"

"Yes," she whispered. She felt weighed down by the pressures he was exerting on her and appalled at his ability to turn everything to suit him. And tired, terribly tired. Her life was going to be purgatory. If Giovanni didn't leave Eternity, she'd have to. "I want to walk home," she said huskily.

"Do what you like. Talk to my mother and let's get this whole sorry business over with fast. I almost have what I want," he said with cold indifference, and reached across her, opening the door, not even leaving the car to do that little courtesy for her as he usually did.

Yes, she thought, he was getting everything he wanted, and that made her spitting mad. On the way back, she sobbed with frustration. Unable to face going home yet, she slipped back into her office at school to catch up on some of the work she'd let pile up on her desk. She began to jam the completed papers on the spike with more malice than ever.

Her hand was hovering over the spike when the phone rang. Grimly she impaled the chit and snatched up the receiver.

"Yes?"

"Where the devil have you been? Get here! Now!"

"Like hell!" she snapped at the arrogant Giovanni.

She had almost dropped the phone on its cradle when she heard him yell, "Adriana!"

"What?" she shouted back.

"She's here! At my house! Come!"

For a brief terrible second, Tina heard a woman's hysterical voice in the background before the line went dead. The whole of her body chilled to ice. With trembling hands she telephoned for a taxi, told everyone in the office that she had to go and spent the short journey rehearsing what she'd say and gnawing her lower lip in anxiety.

"Where is she?" Tina leapt out of the cab, hastily thrust the money at the driver and ran to Giovanni. Oh, God! she thought, panic-stricken at the sight of his white face. He looked terrible!

"Summerhouse," he said tersely.

She ran. He ran. "How?" she yelled.

"Wandering in the garden! Saw me and—" He stumbled, recovered his footing and ran on, dragging her toward the sound of sobbing. "I called for a doctor. She wants you. Help her!" he pleaded when they were just outside the

summerhouse. "For God's sake, I can't stand that weep
ing. Help her, Tina."

"Oh, Gio," she mourned, torn between going to Adri
ana and wanting to stay with him, to help him, too. "G
indoors. Sit down. Breathe deeply. Make some strong cof
fee. I'll be with you soon." She took a backward glance a
his anguished face, the raw black eyes and the terribl
shaking of his body, and walked into the small structure a
calmly as she could.

"Gio!" sobbed Adriana.

Tina took her in her arms and rocked her while she cried
soothing her with gentle strokes and a loving voice. Sh
thought she caught a glimpse of Giovanni in the side win
dow for one brief moment, but when she looked again, he'
gone.

"Gio, Gio!" sobbed Adriana. *"Sono molto contenta..
Andiamo, Tina. Vieni con me?"*

"I don't understand Italian, darling," Tina said softly
"Don't get up. Stay here. The doctor's coming."

Faced with a fresh spasm of helpless weeping, Tina's re
lief was heartfelt when the doctor arrived, sedated Adri
ana, then took her in his car to the hospital. In a flood o
tears, Tina stumbled to the house and called her grandfa
ther from a phone in the hall.

"Thank heaven she's all right! Lal's here—out of he
mind with worry!" he cried in agitation. "Adriana wanted
to come home to see your beau, so Lal brought her back
and then she said something about getting flowers and dis
appeared. We'll go to the hospital. You stay with Gio. He'l
need someone."

"I—I ought to be with Adriana," she mumbled, ashamed
that she felt more anxious now about Giovanni's state o
mind.

"You stay," her grandfather said sternly. "There'll be
enough bodies around the bed as it is. If she's sedated, she
won't need you. Gio does. He must be upset. Talk later."

Gio was hurting. He needed comfort, and all her in
stincts drove her to provide it, because she cared for him so

much and it pained her to think of the shock he'd experienced. His mother had become hysterical upon seeing him. That must be breaking his heart.

All she could offer was her arms, her love, the hope that in time Adriana would accept him again. He had to be patient and wait. Wearily making herself put one foot in front of the other, she went to the nearest door and saw Giovanni standing in the center of the room staring into space as though he'd walked in but had been unable to make his legs take him any farther.

All the love in her heart went out to him. In those hunched shoulders, the tense back, his very stillness, she identified the terrible desolation he felt. And yet when she came quietly to his side and found his unfathomable eyes turned to her, she felt inhibited from offering the comfort she longed to give. It was as if he'd placed a steel wall between them, and however much he ached and cried inside, the message was clear, with ''Don't touch me!'' in every screaming muscle.

''Tea?'' she asked. He shook his head slightly. ''Coffee? Alcohol?''

''No,'' he said in a harsh whisper. His teeth ground together, the black eyes flared with a brief terrible flame and then became bleak and veiled in secrecy once more. ''I can't stay,'' he told her brutally. ''I'll leave town immediately.''

His words were a body blow, and she sank into the nearest chair, a heap of blood and flesh and bone that wanted only one thing—for Giovanni to stay, to be near her so that she could sometimes see him and live on her memories. She loved him more deeply than she'd ever believed possible. And she would go on loving him for the rest of her life.

''The women I love hate me,'' he went on in a low raw tone, and Tina winced. ''They're doing me an injustice. It's crucifying me! I'll go when I've got a little more control. I can't possibly drive now.''

The pain rocked through her, his pain. At that moment she knew he was in such torment that he was speaking without thought and he was speaking the truth. He never drove when upset....

Suddenly, in an explosion of life and hope, it was clear. He didn't drive when upset! He hadn't killed her sister and her little nephew. He'd sworn on his honor that he hadn't been driving. Someone was lying—and it wasn't Giovanni. She believed him. She trusted him. Maybe she couldn't have him as she wanted, but she could at least prove him innocent.

Her loving eyes caressed his brave strong body, and she saw into his vulnerable core with blinding insight. He'd been wronged, especially by her, and she had to put everything right if it took her years. There was an explanation. She sat up straight, forcing steel into her backbone. She'd do it. For him.

"You could stay...." she began.

"What the hell has this place to offer me?" he snarled.

Me, she thought dumbly. *Me*. "Is the house nothing to you? The prize you won?" she tried.

"It's nothing without..." His tongue slicked over his lips, the hooded eyes hid his secrets.

"You wanted revenge and you've got it," she said, working with all the guile she could muster. "Don't you want to stay and enjoy that?"

"I wanted a second chance at finding the love I craved. The fairy-tale ending," he muttered cynically.

"I can swing it even now. Give me two weeks," she said, knowing how much he wanted to be with his mother again.

"Not two minutes!" He strode blindly to the door, but she was there first, barring the way with her body. He grasped her shoulders in a rage that once would have terrified her. "Let me go!" he roared savagely. "Tina, you must let me go!"

"Gio, I believe you," she said quietly, meeting his hostile eyes. "I know you weren't driving your car on the night my sister was killed."

He winced. "Too late. Ten years too late."

"Perhaps. Stay here. In this house. Isn't your mother worth two weeks of your life?" she challenged.

"You bitch!" he seethed angrily. Then, after a long indrawn breath, "Of course she is! God! Two weeks, then. On one condition. I can't— You won't come near me! I don't care what anyone thinks about our engagement. I can't bear this constant togetherness."

"Nor can I," she said, swallowing her own misery. If he hated her so much, she had to accept that. She represented a part of his life he loathed, the lusting hunger he could dispense with once he was married. "I have no intention of coming near you. But I'm almost certain I can unite you with your mother, and then you can both live wherever you like."

She walked out, unable to stand the look on his face. Most of the emotions a good man could possess had spread there in bewildering confusion. Love, tenderness, joy, grief and despair.

For him, his life was about to begin, she vowed. For her, it had ended.

Not wanting to stay indoors, she walked back for her motorbike and drove slowly out to Eternity Point. Where the sea and the endless sky and the vast wilderness soothed her a little, giving her the strength to fight for the good name of the man she loved.

Wandering for what seemed like miles, she came to a deserted part of the beach where she and Giovanni had often sat in silence, just enjoying the view and the clamor of seabirds above the huge dunes that rose like a wall behind her.

She would talk to Beth's parents who'd witnessed the accident and then Beth—all the other witnesses, too. Somewhere there was a weak link—and a liar.

CHAPTER TEN

THREE DAYS LATER, precious days taken as compassionate leave from an astonished principal, Tina threw a weary leg over the seat of her motorbike and limply jabbed at the starter. But inside she was singing, her heart light at last because she had the evidence she needed.

The engine fired and she drove away from Beth, the woman who had ruined Giovanni's life. Beth's parents had been relatively easy to wear down; they felt they'd fallen so far there was nowhere left to go. Beth had been a different matter.

Tina tried not to weep for her friend. She had to stay alert and she was dog tired. On Gio's rules, she shouldn't be driving at all. Oh, God! she thought rawly, what he'd gone through! Yet she had suffered over the past hours, too. Talking, talking, coaxing, mopping tears...

It had been worth it. She'd used all her years of experience in breaking down barriers, inhibitions and lies to get to the truth. Finally, after much persistence, she had forced the admissions from an exhausted and starkly sober Beth. Admissions that had both of them in tears, hugging one another for comfort, the story pouring out of Beth like a suddenly released flood.

Tina decided to drop in on Grandpa first, to say don't wait up, then...then Gio. She smiled softly as she drew up at the garage, thinking how happy Gio would be to know that she could at last make things right between him and his mother.

Six-thirty. Grandpa would be starting supper. Taking the stairs two at a time, she stopped short when she saw the note on the landing.

Adriana missing. No alarm. Bit worried, that's all.
Searching around old home area. Lal doing riverbank.
Usual panic, eh?

Grandpa

Tina groaned and raced downstairs again, crashing smack
into a hard male body. "Gio!" she gasped in a knee-jerk
response, knowing a disappointing instant later that it
wasn't.

"No. Me."

"Jim! I—"

"I screwed up," he muttered awkwardly. "I came to say
sorry. Giovanni had been good to me, but... the keys were
in the ignition and I couldn't resist."

"Jim, I'm glad you've come back, but talk to me later.
We'll work something out," she said, reluctant not to listen
to him when he was so contrite. His nostrils flared at her
rejection, and she laid a gentle hand on his arm. "Adriana's disappeared," she explained. "I'm worried. She's not
safe alone. I have to go and search..."

"The old lady?" Jim frowned. "If you need help, I can
get a few people together to search. Where might she go?"

"The Tamblyn house... anywhere in the town... the
beach..."

"Okay. Got it. We'll cover it all. Don't worry," he said,
seeing her anxious face. "She'll be okay."

"Jim! I'm grateful!" He was all heart—soft as a brush.
Gio *must* take him back! The bike started with a roar. House
or beach? Beach. If Adriana was at the house, Gio would
come across her there. Her teeth snagged her lower lip. More
upsets if he did, she thought gloomily.

The marshes looked vast and unfriendly now, and the
mud flats were suddenly frightening to her worried eyes. The
river stretched out endlessly, glinting with the wicked silvery light of the still-bright sun. But instinct made her head
for the beach.

As she zigzagged up and down the white sand, asking
everyone she came across to keep a lookout for a beautiful

gray-haired lady—perhaps looking lost and vague—she sav
that the sun was lower on the horizon. Dusk was coming.

Perhaps they should get the police, she thought anx
iously. With increasing despair, she stumbled on into th
more deserted part, becoming more frantic with every ex
hausting stretch of beach she covered. It looked intermina
ble. Eternity out there. Please let her be found!

"What the hell are you doing, Tina?"

She whirled at Giovanni's voice and saw him standing b
the distorted bough of a pitch pine, blown horizontal by th
Atlantic gales. "Your mother!" she yelled hysterically
"She's missing!"

He came leaping down to join her at once. "I'll hel|
you!"

"No. We've got a search party. You can't come!" she sai
hotly.

"Because I upset her? Because I've broken her fragil
mind? Is that it, Tina?" he asked hoarsely. "Would she ru
from me, her own son? *Gesù!*" His breath rasped in, ther
out, with one long harsh groan.

She stared at him in sorrow. She'd make it all right fo
him. Later. "She probably would. We can't take that risk
It's going to be...dark soon," she said jerkily. "She'll b
all alone and frightened." *Hold me,* she thought miserably
I want comfort. Show some human care!

"I have to help," he muttered. "I can't do nothing. Yo
must understand that, Tina. If we see her, I'll make mysel
scarce, I swear. Come on," he said urgently. "Better mov
fast."

They scattered surf snipes at the water's edge where the
ran and disturbed sharp-tailed sparrows in the sea lavende
above the high-tide line. Running was easy where the san
was flat but tougher where it was soft. Even with Giovan
ni's strong hand helping her along, she found her leg
growing weaker and weaker.

"I can't go on!" she wailed.

"Rest a moment." His powerful arms hauled her up t
lean beside him against the reservation fence.

Panting heavily, she closed her eyes, feeling the warmth of the dying sun on her lids and the gentle breeze on her cheek, almost like Giovanni's delicate touch. When she opened her eyes again, he was looking at her with the hard blank expression she hated.

"The sun is setting," she said shakily, seeing the red-gold in his hair. Dispiritedly they turned to face the rosy sea. Farther along, two people were wading in water up to their waists. Tina stiffened. One figure was... "Adriana!" she breathed.

"And Jim!" he growled. "*Madonna!* He's dragging her in from the sea!" He began to push himself unsteadily from the fence.

"Bless Jim! No! You can't come!" she warned, as he took a step forward.

His teeth clenched. "I must know she's all right!"

Her heart lurched. "Yes. I'll wave if she's okay. If there's trouble, you'll be the first to know. Look, she seems fine. Wait there. I'll let you know. Oh, Gio!" she said brokenly, wanting to hold him in her arms.

"Go to her. She relates to you," he growled harshly. "If... if Jim's saved her life, tell him I say thank-you. He's got his job back. I'll keep an eye on his progress and make sure he gets due opportunities. And let him know that he's won back the jobs of any students you care to place on work experience."

"Thank you!" she cried, her eyes sparkling. "Gio—"

"Get away from me," he said hoarsely. "I can't bear to be near you."

She hesitated. A quick glance told her that Jim was finding it hard to struggle through the icy water, because he and Adriana were fully clothed.

"We must talk," she said nervously.

"No," he said. "This is the end. It's enough. More than I can bear. I'll send money for a full-time companion for her. I'm leaving Eternity, turning my back on it forever. Eternity. Huh! For God's sake, Tina!" he snarled ferociously. "Go to the person who needs you!"

Miserably, she turned and ran. She heard his soft good-bye, turned, gasping, tried to express the love in her heart, but nothing came from her agonized lips but a harsh groan, and he was already striding away over the rose-colored sand.

She loved him and he was going. He was blameless and didn't know of the chance he had to hold his head up high.

"Gio!" she yelled.

His back stiffened. He whirled around savagely. "No!" he roared. "Let me go, Tina! Leave me in peace!"

The tone, the furious way he spun on his heel and strode away was final. She bit her lip, knowing her duty lay with Adriana. With leaden feet and nothing save numbness in her brain, she staggered to the water, plunging into the sea in a froth of foam and spray. Still some distance out because of the gently shelving shallows, Jim and Adriana forged toward her.

Gio was leaving her. But she had evidence. She must tell him!

"Oh, Gio!" she sobbed. He'd disappear and Adriana would never be reunited with him.

"Tina!" Adriana's wet hand clamped on her arm and then she was locked in a tight embrace.

"Oh Addy! I was so worried!" she wept.

"Don't cry, sweetheart! I am sorry. I had to get away somewhere, to be by myself because my mind was in such a turmoil. This nice young man," said Adriana, smiling up at Jim, "found me trapped on a sandbar."

"What . . . what were you *doing* there?" sniffed Tina.

"I'd been standing there looking out to sea and thinking, and suddenly I was surrounded by water!" said Adriana. "I can swim, but it was cold and I'd have spoiled the nice watch you and Dan gave me for my birthday."

Tina gave Jim a smile of deep gratitude. "Jim, you've been wonderful! Addy," she whispered weakly, hugging her waist as they stumbled through the shallows, "you remembered about the watch!"

"Oh, yes, suddenly I remember a lot of things." She sighed happily.

"Oh, darling, that's wonderful!" said Tina shakily. "Why, for heaven's sake, were you doing your thinking on a sandbar?"

"I was thinking about Gio, what he did...."

"You remember that?" asked Tina, wide-eyed.

"I remember. I tried to sort out how I feel about it now. I'm a little muddled. Your grandpa said you were getting married. Are you marrying Gio?"

Tina's eyes shot to the figure far away in the distance. He looked as lonely as she felt. "No," she said, feeling defeated by life.

"Well, you ought to, and he must talk sense into you," said Adriana firmly. "He loved you more than I've ever known a man to love anyone."

"That's not true," said Tina harshly, astonished at Adriana's recovery. Grandpa had been right. Since the shock of seeing Giovanni, she'd become less and less vague every day.

Adriana's affectionate hand patted Tina's back. "But you love my Gio, don't you, darling?"

"Yes," she muttered, "I do. But he doesn't love me."

"Oh. Who's that up there on the dunes?" Adriana asked innocently.

Tina could see from her twinkling eyes that she knew. "Gio," she said reluctantly.

"Don't you think you ought to tell him I'm all right?" Adriana grinned. "I imagine he'll be worried."

Tina tried to stop gaping. "I—I don't think..." she began hesitantly, her eyes lighting up. She had a chance to catch him and to say that she'd make sure everyone knew he hadn't been driving....

"You go," said Jim briskly. "I'll take Mrs. Kowalski home and keep an eye on her. I'm good with old ladies."

"How lovely," said Adriana happily. "But not so much of the 'old'!"

"I'll tell Gio!" said Tina, her eyes bright with tears. "But why aren't you upset about Gio? You were before."

"Tina, darling, I've been explaining to Jim," she said gently. "Seeing Gio in the garden was such a shock that I found my memory returning. I was crying with happiness, Tina! I wanted us to go to him...."

"You were speaking in Italian!" said Tina in frustration. "I didn't understand you!"

"I know, darling. Nor did the doctor. It was all I could manage at the time till I got over the shock, and then I talked at great length to your grandfather. I know how much you've devoted yourself to me over the past few years. You've been wonderful and I love you for that, Tina. Go to Gio for me," she urged. "Tell him how much I love him."

"But... I'll bring him back to you. You must want to see him, speak to him, hold him...." she said jerkily.

"No. Go now and catch him," said Adriana urgently. "I'm wet through and I'd get pneumonia if I waited here much longer. Tell him Jim's taking me to his home to get me dry and he can come and see me there—but not to rush. I need time to tidy myself. *Run*, child!"

Tina ran, laughing at Adriana's desire to look good for Gio. As if he'd care! Fear that she'd be too late to tell him the good news pumped adrenaline into her blood, giving her weary limbs a new lease on life. He'd been walking slowly and she made good headway, then saw with a sinking heart that he'd reached his car. He'd drive away! Frantically she searched around and picked up a stone, hurling it with all her might and prayers. It hit the car with a satisfying clunk just as he moved off.

"Gio!" she yelled when he jammed on the brakes and leapt out in a tearing fury. "Oh, the fates are with me!" she breathed, falling in exhaustion against the car.

"Look at that!" he roared, pointing to the dent in the trunk. "What the hell are you doing? And why have you abandoned my mother?"

"She told me to." Tina grinned happily.

There was a brief softening of the frozen eyes and an avid hunger crawled into his expression. "You're soaking wet!" he said hoarsely.

"So's your mother. That's why she's making her way to Jim's car, closer up the beach," she said gently. "He's taking her back to his place to dry off before... before she sees you!'' she cried, eyes shining. ''She's better, Gio!'' she said tremulously. ''She recognizes you—''

''Oh, God!'' he groaned.

''And says she loves you and will be waiting for you.'' Her loving eyes took in his start of disbelief, how he searched her face for the truth and, when he'd found it, believed it, how his smile became so broad and happy she could hardly speak. ''You were right and I was wrong,'' she went on. ''Your appearance was all she needed to bring her memory function back. She loves you. You have your mother's love and I'm very, very happy for you both. You have to stay now—''

''I can't!'' he said rawly.

''You can,'' she said, love filling her eyes. ''Perhaps if she has you, it will make it easier for her when I go.''

''What do you mean, when you go?'' he demanded.

Sadly she smiled, reached out and touched his chest. He stepped back warily. ''I love you,'' she said, offering him her whole heart in those three words. ''That's why I have to go. It would make things too awkward for everyone. Grandpa and I can find a house somewhere else. Perhaps Rockport.''

''Why?'' he asked hoarsely.

''One day you'll get married. I can't bear to think of you with another woman, let alone see you with someone else. I know it's wicked to feel like that, but I do. I'd rather shut my mind off. I have always loved you and never, ever have felt anything different. Even when I thought you were a coward, I still loved you and that's why the thought of you lying to save your own skin hurt so much. So very much.''

''You *thought* I was a coward?'' he asked, his eyes narrowed.

''I went to see Beth's parents,'' she said huskily. ''They've come down in the world.'' Her lashes flicked up, her eyes anxious. ''That wasn't your doing, was it?''

''No,'' he said curtly. ''I believe her father had something of a breakdown and went through a period of investing unwisely.''

She bit her lip hard and lifted her small anxious face to his. It was iron hard, without expression. "They are so unhappy," she said sadly. "I think they wish they'd told the truth long ago."

"The . . . truth?" His eyes were riveted to hers.

"Yes. I explained why I was there and they told me everything. It confirmed the story you gave, Gio," she said softly. "They said they saw you driving past very slowly because Beth was leaning over and thrashing her arms around, hitting out at you in hysteria. They saw you trying to keep control of the car, then you swerved and almost crashed into the pedestrian who was one of the witnesses. You stopped the car, threw the keys at Beth and walked away. After a moment she . . . she drove the car at you. . . .'

Tina couldn't go on. She felt herself being drawn to Giovanni's breast, to comfort, to his heart. Gratefully she laid her head on his chest and struggled to get her emotions under control again.

"I jumped out of the way. Beth skidded and hit your sister's car," he said grimly, continuing the story she now knew by heart. "God! It was like watching my uncle die all over again! I had my hand on the door handle of Sue's car when I saw my fuel tank had been fractured and was spilling fuel everywhere."

"Beth said you jumped back into your car and pushed her out of the way. . . ."

"She wouldn't move!" he said hoarsely. "She was rigid with shock. I had to act fast, had to be rough. I yanked open her door and pushed her out then reversed the car to prevent it exploding and setting fire to Sue and . . . and little Mike. God! It was a nightmare!" he groaned. "I'll never forget it as long as I live."

"Then the crowd surrounded you," she finished. "And the accusations began. Now Beth's parents will testify and so will she. Your name will be cleared."

"Beth? But . . ."

"She and her parents have all been in a living hell since you were imprisoned," Tina said gently. "The guilt had eaten into them like a cancer. You were right about Beth being an alcoholic. I persuaded them all that psychoanaly-sis wouldn't get any of them anywhere until they'd faced up to their responsibilities. I told Beth she owed me, as a friend, because I love you, and I want everyone to know you didn't kill Sue and Mike. I asked Geoff Kent on the phone what would happen to her, and he said he thought the court would be lenient. But I don't think Beth cares. All she wants is to set the record straight. I told her she's young enough to start her life over, with a fresh page.''

"Tina," he said chokingly, "you did this for me? Even though . . . ?''

"So—" she smiled brightly, happy for him "—I won't stay around, Gio. I won't make it difficult for you to start a new life. I'll . . . go.''

"Tina! This is ridiculous!'' he said in astonishment. "You are my new life! We're engaged, remember? The arrange-ments are under way. You wear my ring.'' He gripped her arms tightly, his mouth firm. "No woman runs out on me!''

Her eyes rounded and flickered with pain. "No! I won't marry you! I won't honor some damn Sicilian agreement just because of your pride.''

"Pride?'' He gave a husky laugh. "Would you accept my undying love, instead?'' he asked in amusement. "Tina! You fool, you wonderful, fierce, uncompromising, brave fool! Everyone in the whole of Eternity knows I worship the dust beneath your feet. Haven't you an inkling of that? What do I have to do to show you?''

"You loved Beth,'' she said stiffly. "It was that, and her story about your begging her to sleep with you, crawling to her like some devoted slave, that wore me down after the accident,'' she said miserably. "I did stick up for you, but everyone kept saying you were a bastard because of the way you'd treated me, and I began to believe them! You still do love her, I think,'' she added, feeling wretched.

"I never have. On my honor,'' he murmured. Tina looked up, her eyes bright with unshed tears. Giovanni smiled at her fondly. "Did she say nothing about our argument?'' he asked gently.

"Yes. You'd asked her to persuade her father to fund part of your Harvard fees—"

"No. That's a lie," he said. "We had a fight because I was rejecting her. My darling, she couldn't believe I'd do such a thing. *She* dumped guys, not the other way around. She felt she'd lost face when I left her for you. All those rumors about me being crazy about her were just not true."

"So what happened?" Tina asked quietly.

"That fatal night, she accosted me in the diner and demanded to talk to me in private. When we got in the car, she started to flirt with me. I told her I was in love with you and she flipped out." He scowled, the deep red sky making an angry blaze of his windswept blond hair. "I was offered money and marriage. I said I couldn't be bought, she got physical, and I flung the car keys at her and got out."

"You weren't two-timing?" Tina asked, holding her breath for his answer.

"Of course not!" he answered. "Initially I'd dated her because she was the school catch, the ice maiden who'd never succumbed to any guy," he said ruefully, settling his arms more firmly around her. "I found out why. She hates sex. More than that, she's a controller. She controlled you, Tina, but you were too generous and kind to realize that. She's love starved, a poor little rich girl, who doesn't know how to love, a woman with the face of an angel and a heart of ice. You, on the other hand, are warm and loving and have a heart of gold. I fell for you so hard I walked on air when you said you'd date me."

"But...when you came back and threw those coins at me, you...you treated me like dirt!" she said uncertainly.

"I'd intended to. Fate made things turn out a little differently, and I was furious with myself for finding you so appealing," he admitted wryly. "I'd returned to win back my mother and to show you my contempt and give you a hard time, and there you were, looking more beautiful and seductive than I'd ever remembered. I couldn't stop looking at you, touching you any way I could. I hated you for tearing up the plans I'd written inside my head. I wanted to hurt you, I wanted to love you, I wanted sex.... Oh, God! How I wanted all those things!''

"You even told me you loved me," she said softly, savoring the memory with a smile.

"At Marion's shop? I did," he said in a low tone. "And I meant it with every fiber of my being, Tina."

"Gio!" she whispered, shaken by the conviction in his voice. She gazed into his eyes and saw the truth. It was in every line of his face, each and every tensed muscle. Joy began to curl with delicious slowness through her body.

He smiled down at her. "It was an ironic twist that had me buying you an engagement ring and swearing my undying love when I really did. You'd confused me with your contradictory signals. I was certain you felt *something* for me, and I dared to believe I could get us back together again. But you stubbornly refused to say you loved me—at least not the way I wanted to hear it!"

"Why did you say you didn't want anything to do with me and then that you were leaving?" she asked in a small voice, remembering the anguish she'd felt.

"Because I couldn't stand to be near you and yet not to be loved by you. I couldn't bear to see you but not touch you, or love you, or shower my feelings on you. It hurt too much. So very, very much."

"I understand," she said, hugging him tightly. "That's exactly how I felt. It was the reason I decided to leave."

"And all these years," he marveled, "you and your grandfather have cared for my mother!"

"I love her," she said shakily. "She's adorable."

"We'll both love her," he murmured into her tumbled hair. "If they want to, your grandfather and my mother and Lal can come to live with us. Your parents, too, if they want to come back. At least, they must visit. Attend our wedding."

Shyly she shot a glance at him from under her lashes. "A wedding! A wedding in Eternity—in the chapel...."

"It's all half arranged, isn't it?" He laughed softly, kissing her frown lines. "I've got the file cards!"

"Idiot!" She giggled.

"My darling, Tina," he murmured. "Now we can go ahead with the wedding, the youth center...."

"I thought of study rooms for students like Ethan," she remembered.

He chuckled and ruffled her hair affectionately. "Yes, yes. Now, for a while," he said sternly, "you have to forget worrying about other people and think of your own selfish needs. Turn your mind to flower girls. Guest lists. Our wedding day."

"Our wedding day!" she repeated, hugging herself in delight. "And...can I be selfish and tell you that I'm hungry?" she asked innocently. Giovanni looked disconcerted, and she looked up at him with wickedly alluring eyes. "I was thinking we could go back and pick up five tubs of ice cream on the way," she said huskily.

"Five's a bit much!"

"Depends what you do with them."

A shudder ran through him and she thought she detected happy tears in his glistening dark eyes. "So it does. What...what flavor?" he asked roughly.

"Pistachio, toffee, tutti-frutti— Gio! What are you—?" She couldn't finish, for he'd pulled her to the ground and begun to kiss her passionately.

"Tina, I love you so very much," he said. "I have to hold you, kiss you...."

They clung together in silence, not moving for a while as the overwhelming emotions claimed them both. Tina shut her eyes and let her fingers twine in his beautifully soft hair, her mind full of dreams.

"Eternity Point," she murmured reflectively. He stroked her hair with a loving and gentle hand.

There was no need for words. They knew the old legend. On Eternity Point, lovers had made their commitments to one another for as far back as anyone could remember.

"To Eternity," said Giovanni quietly. And Tina nestled against him, filled with the wonderful certainty of deep love and the joy of knowing there was a lifetime ahead with the man she adored.

IT'S FREE! IT'S FUN! ENTER THE

☆ "Hooray for ☆
☆ Hollywood" ☆

SWEEPSTAKES!

We're giving away prizes to celebrate the screening of four new romance movies on CBS TV this fall! Look for the movies on four Sunday afternoons in October. And be sure to return your Official Entry Coupons to try for a fabulous vacation in Hollywood!

⭐ If you're the Grand Prize winner we'll fly you and your companion to Los Angeles for a 7-day/6-night vacation you'll never forget!

⭐ You'll stay at the luxurious Regent Beverly Wilshire Hotel,* a prime location for celebrity spotting!

⭐ You'll have time to visit Universal Studios,* stroll the Hollywood Walk of Fame, check out celebrities' footprints at Mann's Chinese Theater, ride a trolley to see the homes of the stars, and more!

⭐ The prize includes a rental car for 7 days and $1,000.00 pocket money!

Someone's going to win this fabulous prize, and it might just be you! Remember, the more times you enter, the better your chances of winning!

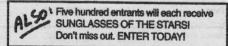
The proprietors of the trademark are not associated with this promotion.

CBSIBC

Take 4 bestselling love stories FREE

Plus get a FREE surprise gift!

HARLEQUIN®

Weddings, Inc.

If you enjoyed visiting Eternity, Massachusetts, and meeting the people of Weddings, Inc., Harlequin would like to invite you to even more weddings! Just collect three (3) proofs-of-purchase from the backs of any of the Weddings, Inc. titles and Harlequin will send you a free short-story collection featuring weddings!

Just select the book you would like, fill in the order form and send it, along with three (3) proofs-of-purchase for each book ordered, plus $2.25 postage and handling, to: WEDDINGS, INC., P.O. Box 9071, Buffalo, NY 14269-9071 or P.O. Box 604, Fort Erie, Ontario L2A 5X3.

☐	#83228-6	WITH THIS RING	(1487)
☐	#83238-6	TO HAVE AND TO HOLD	(1488)
☐	#83258-3	JUST MARRIED	(1489)
☐	#83295-5	MARRIAGE BY DESIGN	(1490)

Name:_____

Address:_____

_____ City:_____

State/Prov.:_____ Zip/Postal Code: _____

(Please allow 4-6 weeks for delivery. Offer expires January 31, 1995.)

WED-POPR

ONE PROOF-OF-PURCHASE

097 KCC

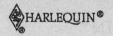 HARLEQUIN® 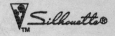 Silhouette®

The movie event of the season can be the reading event of the year!

Lights… The lights go on in October when CBS presents Harlequin/Silhouette Sunday Matinee Movies. These four movies are based on bestselling Harlequin and Silhouette novels.

Camera… As the cameras roll, be the first to read the original novels the movies are based on!

Action… Through this offer, you can have these books sent directly to you! Just fill in the order form below and you could be reading the books…before the movie!

48288-4	Treacherous Beauties by Cheryl Emerson $3.99 U.S./$4.50 CAN.	☐
83305-9	Fantasy Man by Sharon Green $3.99 U.S./$4.50 CAN.	☐
48289-2	A Change of Place by Tracy Sinclair $3.99 U.S./$4.50CAN.	☐
83306-7	Another Woman by Margot Dalton $3.99 U.S./$4.50 CAN.	☐

TOTAL AMOUNT	$	
POSTAGE & HANDLING	$	
($1.00 for one book, 50¢ for each additional)		
APPLICABLE TAXES*	$	_____
TOTAL PAYABLE	$	_____
(check or money order—please do not send cash)		

To order, complete this form and send it, along with a check or money order for the total above, payable to Harlequin Books, to: **In the U.S.:** 3010 Walden Avenue, P.O. Box 9047, Buffalo, NY 14269-9047; **In Canada:** P.O. Box 613, Fort Erie, Ontario, L2A 5X3.

Name: _____

Address: _____ City: _____

State/Prov.: _____ Zip/Postal Code: _____

*New York residents remit applicable sales taxes.
 Canadian residents remit applicable GST and provincial taxes.

CBSPR